Medical Astrology

Blank pagae

Medical Astrology

Dr Prem Kumar Sharma

Rupa & Co

Copyright © Dr Prem Kumar Sharma 2009

Published 2009 by

Rupa & Co

7/16, Ansari Road, Daryaganj,
New Delhi 110 002

Sales Centres:

Allahabad Bangalooru Chandigarh Chennai
Hyderabad Jaipur Kathmandu
Kolkata Mumbai

Typeset by
Mindways Design
1410 Chiranjiv Tower
43 Nehru Place
New Delhi 110 019

Printed in India by
Rekha Printers Pvt Ltd.
A-102/1, Okhla Industrial Area, Phase-II,
New Delhi-110 020

Hail to the Divine Mother!

Blank pagae

CONTENTS

Section C: Cure

PREFACE

Since ancient times in India, as well as in other parts of the world, astrology has been used in the medical practice. In India, the *vaids* or traditional medical doctors of the old school of Ayurveda used to cast a horoscope of the patient to analyse the causes of the disease and to prescribe the cure.

The seventeenth century herbalist Nicholas Culpeper once said, 'Only astrologers are fit to study medicine and a medical man without astrology is like a lamp without oil.' I am aware of the availability of many books on this subject, both by Indian as well as foreign authors. Usually in these books, the diseases and their astrological indications are described but rarely any book defines health and discusses the topic in detail.

The dictionary defines health as 'the state of wellness in body and mind'. This definition is a good attempt because it includes 'mind' and we all realise sooner or later that our mind plays a crucial and decisive role in our feelings of wellness and cure of diseases. But we of the East, due to our very rich spiritual background, know that a very essential factor is still missing in the above definition of health.

To clarify my point of view, I quote below a verse from a pioneer Ayurvedic treatise namely *Shushruta Samhita.*

Samdosha smaginshach samdhatumalkriyah,
prasanntmendriymana swasth iteybhidhiatey.

The above verse translates: 'If the three humours called *doshas* are balanced, the fire of life called *agni* is in a healthy state, and the good state of tissues and the metabolic end-products give a balanced state of senses, mind and spirit, then all these lead to good health.'

My in-depth study of the Vedas and other treatises has inspired me to present a book on medical astrology. I have included a full chapter on the topic of health under the light of astrology.

I hope my humble attempt on health issues and its related remedies will provide inspiration to the readers. I also believe that if you follow the guidelines in this book, you will discover renewed health, happiness and contentment.

Dr Prem Kumar Sharma

INTRODUCTION

A human being is a product of three main parts, viz., body, mind and soul. So to enjoy good health, one needs to be aware of these three elements.

As per astrology, the physical body is represented by the ascendant of the birth chart, the mind by the Moon, and the soul by the Sun. Therefore, we can conclude that the ascendant lord, Moon and Sun in a chart, decide broadly the health of a person.

I believe that when there is imbalance of harmony among these three, then disease sets in. Above all, the strength and auspiciousness of the Sun in a chart is the greatest asset as far as physical health is concerned.

The favourable ascendant lord and the Sun gives self-confidence, self-reliance, recuperative powers and healing powers; and all these are very essential for perfect sparkling health.

Then follows the role of the mind for which an affliction-free and strong Moon ensures a right mental balance in order to remain happy even in adverse conditions. A strong and balanced mind also helps you recover fast from illness. All my beliefs are based on my experiences and astrological predictions, which have been proved correct time after time over the past decades.

I have divided this book into three sections. The first, which is Section-A, contains nine chapters through which I have tried to give all the concepts and information about the subject of medical astrology. Then in Section-B, which consists of eleven chapters, I have discussed diseases of the body and mind. The Section-C is about cure, contains a chapter on the remedial measures. Now let us see in a nutshell what this book is all about.

I have started the first section with a chapter on 'Healthy Living'. In this chapter I have explained health through a broader perspective, which contains the physical, emotional, intellectual, spiritual, occupational and social aspects.

The second chapter is about 'Longevity' or in other words, the life span of a person. The four main longevity categories are explained and astrological indications about these are described in this chapter.

The next four chapters, viz., Chap. 3-6 describe the relevance of planets, signs, houses and constellations respectively as regard to the body parts and diseases which these represent.

The seventh chapter explains the role and importance of the ascendant of a chart in the light of medical astrology. The sixth house in a chart is the main house, which signifies disease. An analysis of this house is described here.

The last chapter of Section-A 'Locating Vulnerable Body Parts' and will help you predict the body parts and possible ailments of these, which the native may expect during the periods of the relevant planets.

The Section-B contains eleven chapters – 'Head Diseases', 'Eye Diseases', 'Ear, Nose and Throat (ENT) Diseases', 'Nervous System Diseases', 'Chest Diseases', 'Abdomen Diseases' 'Reproductive System Diseases', 'Diseases of Legs and Feet', 'Cancer', 'Skin Diseases' and 'Miscellaneous Diseases'. The last section – Section-C, contains a chapter in which remedial measures have been described in detail.

Astrology is a science but it differs from other sciences in many ways; and one such way is the interpretation of the astrological indications. Herein comes the role of an astrologer and his depth of knowledge. I have expressed my views here and I respect other's views as well. I believe that nobody's opinion is entirely worthless. Even a clock, which is stopped, and not working, gives accurate time twice daily.

I hope my humble effort brings happiness, contentment and good health to all my sincere readers who have faith in me.

Dr Prem Kumar Sharma

Blank page

SECTION A
Concepts and Data

1

HEALTHY LIVING

The Hindi word for health is *swaasthya*, which means *'swayam mein sthit'* or established in the self. Dwelling in one's own self is possible only when one is at peace with the self and the environment, and that is a state of true health.

In the absolute sense, having perfect health is very rare. As long as we are governed by desires we can never be fully satisfied and healthy. Only a self-realised person who has risen above the physical desires and mental turmoil can be called a truly healthy person.

Our great ancient *rishi*s, propounded the Indian system of medicine called Ayurveda. They were not just ordinary people but spiritually very knowledgeable individuals who could see the aura and had an in-depth knowledge of astrology. They knew that each individual is genetically different and had a unique constitution and nature *(prakriti).* Therefore, they recommended casting a birth chart of the person to analyse and locate the cause of disease and then suggesting a cure. The astrological information was used along with the knowledge of a person's predominating dosha or humour.

The western medical world boasts of its modern day achievements in the field of surgery whereas the humble but rich ancient Indian culture is a storehouse of original pioneering knowledge, which has inspired the modern day western scientists and doctors and given them valuable ideas.

Sushruta was a renowned surgeon of ancient India during sixth century BC. He is also the author of a well-known treatise Sushruta Samhita. This treatise describes about three hundred surgical procedures and about 120 surgical instruments.

Astrologically speaking, the ascendant and its lord are the most important factors for determining one's health in general. Thereafter comes the function of the Sun and Moon. The Moon is as important as the ascendant because of its special consideration in astrology. Also the Moon being the *karaka* or significator for mind plays a crucial and decisive role in the mental state of a person.

Self-confidence, equanimity, tranquillity and positive outlook play an important role in not only keeping one relaxed and free from undue worries, but these also help to enjoy good health.

If you suffer from some disease due to essential conditions of life style, then you need a strong and positive mental outlook and equanimity in order to progress in life in spite of the diseased condition.

Let us ask ourselves again the same question, 'What is health?' and go a bit deeper to find the answer. We realise that we do not exist just on the physical plane but we have a complex personality which touches the mental as well as spiritual planes also. This knowledge helps us redefine health as a sort of integration of body, mind and soul. Keeping in mind the fact that we live in a society and cannot exist without the aid of others, let us broaden the horizons of the above views by including the following aspects:

1. Physical
2. Emotional
3. Intellectual
4. Spiritual
5. Occupational
6. Social

So, if we consider all the above-mentioned six aspects and take care of these in our daily life, then we can make sure that we enjoy health and wellness in the true sense. Let us now describe each of these aspects.

1. Physical: Our physical body needs a good supply of minerals, vitamins, fats, carbohydrates and proteins in the form of a balanced daily diet which includes vegetables, fruits, pulses, wheat, water, fruit juices, milk and dairy products.

In addition to a balanced diet our physical body needs regular exercise as well. If you suffer from some heart or lung ailment then consult your physician before choosing an exercise. A morning or evening walk is the safest and the most effective exercise for all age groups.

While we are talking about the physical, there are two most important items which need our attention. The first of these is sleep. A good sound sleep is very important for all of us. Sleeping habits influence our physical, mental as well as spiritual development. Lack of sleep or disturbed sleep can make one irritable or touchy and also vulnerable to diseases.

The second important factor is avoiding constipation. Regular bowel clearance is a must to be healthy and fit. Constipation makes one giddy, lethargic, dull, unenthusiastic and prone to various diseases.

In your birth chart, analyse the condition of the ascendant and its lord, the Sun and the Moon. Try to boost up their strength if any of these is weak. If these are under afflictions then follow the remedial measures given in Section-C for propitiation of the afflicted planets.

2. Emotional: The emotional side of our personality can overshadow other aspects as it carries a strong influence. First of all, try to analyse your emotional character by regular introspection and objective approach.

Discover your emotional secrets. You are the best judge of your own emotional nature and requirements. This can help you keep yourself in an emotionally balanced state of mind.

Remember that irritation and unpleasantness to a certain degree exists in nearly everyone's life. Take things by not just habitually reacting to situations, but rather acting intelligently and wisely so that you keep a balanced outlook.

If you find it difficult to achieve emotional balance then get your birth chart analysed and find out the reasons and an effective cure. The Moon and Venus need propitiation if under afflictions and a boost if weak in strength. These are the main planets, which are related to our emotional behaviour.

3. Intellectual: This implies using one's intellect or brain in one's activities and interaction with others. Each one of us has a different level of intellectual development. Also not everyone is engaged in intellectual pursuits. Using your intellect in your day-to-day activities means living conscientiously and not just following things with blind faith. The habit of using one's intellect will also automatically develop the intellect. Life is to be lived intelligently irrespective of your station in life.

The Mercury is the significator of intellect. It is quite delicate in the sense that it becomes malefic if it comes under conjunct influences by a malefic planet.

4. Spiritual: Our spiritual personality is the real core of our being around which the physical level of existence revolves from life to life. Unless we devote some time and energy daily for understanding our basic spiritual nature and needs we fail to see things in perspective. We also fail to understand the real nature of things and the plan of god and our own destiny.

The Sun and Jupiter are to be taken care of for all-round spiritual development. The Sun represents the soul, which is the very core of our personality. The Jupiter governs wisdom, righteousness, spiritual stature and religious bent of mind.

5. Occupational: Each one of us is engaged in some occupation or profession. Basically we need some occupation to fulfil our monetary requirements. But selecting an occupation depending upon our education, natural gifts, skills and talents, etc., gives us more satisfaction and a meaningful lifestyle.

Try to boost the planet controlling your occupational work. A deeper analysis of your birth chart is needed for determining the significators of your profession. In this regard the author's book, *The Stars and Your Profession*, published by *Rupa & Co* will be helpful.

6. Social: It was rightly remarked by Aristotle that man is a social animal. Living at the selfish level does not give dynamism to our personality. Caring for others and forming long-time relations within and outside the family gives us social wellness and a purposeful existence.

In the birth chart the Third house is mainly responsible for our social contacts and relations. The significator planet is the Mercury.

Cheerfulness – key to good health

The great sage Socrates was condemned to death by the ignorant rulers of that time because they presumed that he was misguiding the people. He was asked to prepare for death. In response to this message the great sage smiled and said that by never doing any wrong to anyone throughout his life he has already prepared himself for death and he shall accept it happily.

It is a fact that if you never do any harm to anyone then you need not fear anyone. Fearlessness leads to cheerfulness and to health. There is no cosmetic like cheerfulness to make you beautiful and no such tonic to keep you healthy. An experiment was conducted in an American university on 193 subjects in the age group of twenty-one to fifty-five years. It was observed that those who were generally confident, optimist and cheerful had a strong immune system as compared to those who were pessimistic and depressed.

2

LONGEVITY

Each of us has a deep-seated desire to live a long life of happiness and prosperity. We also wish that all our dear ones enjoy a long life.

Maximum lifespan and its division

According to one belief the maximum life span or *pooran aayu* is considered as hundred years. As per this belief, the total lifespan of a person is divided into four divisions as follows:

1. *Balarishtha* or infant mortality – First eight years comes under this category.
2. *Alp aayu* or short lifespan – Between eight years to thirty-two years.
3. *Madhyam aayu* or medium lifespan – This is thirty-two to sixty-four years.

4. Pooran aayu or full lifespan – The lifespan from sixty-four to hundred years is considered as full lifespan.

The other belief is based on *vimshotri dasha* system of *Maharishi Parashara* according to which the total lifespan is 120 years instead of hundred years. The author also supports the latter system where the last two divisions get modified as, Madhyam aayu is from thirty-two to seventy-five years and Pooran aayu is from seventy-five to 120 years.

Death inflicting planets or *marak grehas*

The Second and Seventh houses in a chart are called *marak sthanas* or the death inflicting houses. The logic behind this is explained below.

The Eighth house in the birth chart represents longevity or the span of life. According to the principle of *bhavaat bhavam niyaye* the Eighth from the Eighth house, viz., the Third house also represents the longevity of the native. In fact, the above principle states that whatever a house at certain number of places from the ascendant signifies the house at same number of places from that house signifies the same significations. Also we know that the Twelfth house from any house is the house of loss to that house. If we apply this later principle to the two houses of longevity, viz., Third and Eighth then the houses Second and Seventh being the Twelfth from Third and Eighth respectively, are the houses of loss of longevity or in other words the death inflicting or *maraka* houses.

Planets related to these maraka houses during their periods can either give death or suffering due to disease. In addition to the lords of these two houses there are also other death inflicting planets.

We give below a comprehensive list of all planets that can either cause death of the native during their main or sub-periods or can cause extreme suffering due to some disease.

1. Lords of Second and Seventh houses.
2. Planets particularly malefics posited in Second and Seventh houses.
3. Planets particularly malefics conjunct Second and Seventh lords.
4. Even benefics conjunct Second and Seventh lords.
5. Third and Eighth lords particularly when they are weak.
6. Third or Eighth lords particularly when conjunct Second or Seventh lords.
7. Saturn when associated with any of the above.
8. The Sixth lord.
9. The weakest planet of the chart even if it is the ascendant lord.

Apart from the above, the following known as *chchidra greha* (planets which act like a perforation in the pot of life) can also cause death or suffering.

1. The Eighth lord.
2. Planet posited in the Eighth house.

3. Planet aspecting the Eighth house.
4. The lord of the Twenty-second *dreshkaan* (If we divide the degrees into ten degree parts called dreshkaan then counting from the first dreshkaan from the beginning of the ascendant, see where the Twenty-second dreshkaan falls).
5. Planet conjunct Eighth lord.
6. The lord of the Sixty-fourth *navamsha.*
7. That planet which is fast enemy of Eighth lord.

So, one needs to analyse the *dasha/antardasha* (main and sub-periods) of the above death-inflicting planets for estimating the probable time of death or suffering.

The author would like to clarify that the death occurs during the estimated life span division, viz., alp, madhyam or pooran when any of the above planetary periods are operating. Until that has not reached the periods of any of the above-mentioned death-inflicting (marak) planets, it may cause disease or mental or physical suffering instead of death.

General assessment of longevity

Although, exact calculation of lifespan years is beyond the scope of present-day astrology, yet, a dependable general view regarding the lifespan category, viz., alp, madhyam or pooran can be made from the analysis of the chart. There are some distinct yogas or planetary combinations which indicate a particular lifespan category, some of these are given in this chapter.

It is generally observed that the placement of benefic planets in square and trine houses and malefic planets in Third, Sixth and Eleventh houses and the strong Moon, Sun, ascendant lord and the Moon sign lord confer pooran aayu to the native.

Therefore, one needs to observe how many of the above constituents including the Eighth house, its lord and significator Saturn are weak and afflicted and thereby reduce the lifespan.

Estimating the lifespan

Here is a method for estimating the lifespan, although, it is not a foolproof method, yet if employed along with the results of other indications, may help to make final decision regarding longevity:

From the birth chart of the native, let us observe in which signs the constituents of the following three cases fall:

1. (a) Ascendant lord   (b) Eighth lord
2. (a) Ascendant   (b) Moon
3. (a) Moon   (b) Saturn

In each of the above three cases one can determine the lifespan division using the following Table 2.1:

Table 2.1: Table for determining the life span category.

Sign of one constituent	Sign of other constituent	Resulting lifespan category
Aries, Cancer, Libra, Capricorn	Taurus, Leo, Scorpio, Aquarius	Madhyam aayu or medium life span thirty-two to seventy-five years
Aries, Cancer, Libra, Capricorn	Gemini, Virgo, Sagittarius, Pisces	Alp aayu or short lifespan up to thirty-two years
Taurus, Leo, Scorpio, Aquarius	Gemini, Virgo, Sagittarius, Pisces	Pooran aayu or full lifespan seventy-five to 125 years

If in a case both constituents fall under the same sign then decide as below:

If in Aries, Cancer, Libra, Capricorn then pooran aayu or full lifespan.

If in Taurus, Leo, Scorpio, Aquarius then alp aayu or short lifespan.

And if in Gemini, Virgo, Sagittarius, Pisces then madhyam aayu or medium lifespan.

The concluding lifespan category will be the one which appears in at least two out of the above three cases. But in case, if all the three cases show different lifespan categories then the decision indicated by the following Fourth case will be the final:

4.   (a) Ascendant (b) *hora lagan*

Determining the hora lagan: In order to calculate the hora lagan we assume the following data:

Time of birth: 13:25:00 hours, sunrise time on the date of birth at the place of birth: 07:18 hours, IST, longitude of the Sun in the birth chart: 7^S: $13°:57'$

Now subtract the sunrise time from the birth time:

Time of birth	=	13:25:00
Sunrise time	=	07:18:00
Difference	=	06:07:00

There is a unique way of converting this time difference into longitude in terms of sign: degrees: minutes. For this, divide the minute's figure of the time difference by 2.

7 minutes ÷ 2 = 3 minutes: 30 seconds

So we rewrite the difference as = 6:03:30, now add this to the longitude of the Sun as below:

Longitude of Sun	=	7^S: 13º:57'
Add difference	=	6 : 03 :30
Hora lagan	=	13^S: 17º:21' as the sign figure is more than 12 subtract 12
Subtract 12^S	=	01^S: 17º:21'

Therefore, the hora lagan of Taurus 17º:21

In order to clarify the above-explained method consider the birth chart 2.1 of the example 2.1 given in this chapter.

Observing the following:

1. (a) Ascendant lord   (b) Eighth lord
2. (a) Ascendant   (b) Moon
3. (a) Moon   (b) Saturn

Observing the signs of the above constituents from the birth chart 2.1 we get as below:

1. (a) Scorpio   (b) Scorpio
2. (a) Libra   (b) Leo
3. (a) Leo   (b) Capricorn

Interpreting these signs in terms of the lifespan categories as given in the above table we get as below:

1. Alp aayu
2. Madhyam aayu
3. Madhyam aayu

Therefore, the lifespan category indicated for this native is madhyam aayu that between thirty-two to seventy-five years.

Yogas indicating alp aayu (short lifespan)

The following situations indicate alp aayu:

1. Weak ascendant lord having no association with benefic planets and posited in Sixth, Eighth or Twelfth house.
2. The ascendant lord and the Eighth lord having conjunctions with or aspects of malefic planets.

3. If the ascendant, Eighth lord, Tenth lord and Saturn all are weak.

4. If Saturn is posited in the Eighth house, Mars in the Fifth house and Ketu in the ascendant.

5. If malefic planets are posited in Sixth, Eighth and Twelfth houses.

6. If the Sun, Moon and Mars are posited in the Seventh house and Saturn in the ascendant.

7. If the Eighth lord is posited in the ascendant along with Ketu.

8. If the Moon is conjunct with malefic planets and malefic planets are posited in the ascendant.

9. If the Eighth lord is posited in a square house and the ascendant lord is weak.

10. If the Moon is conjunct a malefic planet and posited in Fifth, Seventh, Eighth, Ninth or Twelfth house.

11. If the ascendant lord is conjunct Eighth lord.

12. If the ascendant lord is posited in the Eighth house and it is conjunct with or aspected by a malefic planet and the Eighth lord is in the Eleventh house.

13. If there are no benefic planets posited in square houses and malefic planets are posited in the ascendant and Eighth house and the weak Moon is in the Twelfth house.

14. If benefic planets are posited in the Third and Eighth houses and these are also under affliction.

15. Placement of the Eighth lord in the ascendant and the ascendant lord in the Eighth house.

Yogas indicating madhyam aayu (medium lifespan)

The following situations indicate madhyam aayu:

1. If all the benefic planets are posited in malefic houses, Saturn is in the ascendant, Moon in the Fourth house, Mars in the Seventh and the Sun in the Tenth house.
2. If Saturn is posited in the ascendant and the Moon in the Eighth or Twelfth house.
3. If the Third or Sixth lord is posited in a square house.
4. If at least any two out of the lords of Eighth, Eleventh ascendant and Tenth house are very strong.
5. Placement of the Mercury, Jupiter and Venus in the Second, Third and Eleventh houses.
6. If in the chart of Aries ascendant, the malefic planets are in square houses and Jupiter is in the Eighth house.
7. If evil planets are placed in the Second, Third, Fourth, Fifth, Eighth and Eleventh houses.
8. If Jupiter is posited in a square or trine house, the ascendant lord is weak and malefic planets are placed in the Sixth, Eighth and Twelfth houses.
9. If any two out of the ascendant lord, Eighth lord, Tenth lord and Saturn are strong.
10. If weak Moon is posited in the ascendant and is in the *navamsha* of Saturn.
11. If the Sun is conjunct Rahu and aspected by malefic planets.
12. If the Eighth lord is in the ascendant in a fixed sign, viz., Taurus, Leo, Scorpio or Aquarius and there is no benefic planet in the Eighth house.

13. If Jupiter is posited in the Third or Eleventh house, Venus in the Fifth or Ninth house and both are conjunct with or aspected by malefic planets.
14. If the Mercury is posited in a square house in its sign of exaltation, friendly sign or own sign and a strong planet is in a square house and the Moon is posited in the Seventh house and aspected by Jupiter.
15. If Mars is posited in Eighth or Twelfth house in a fixed sign, viz., Taurus, Leo, Scorpio or Aquarius.

Yogas indicating pooran aayu (full lifespan)

The following situations indicate pooran aayu:

1. If Venus is posited in a square house, the Moon and Jupiter are posited in the ascendant in cancer sign and the Eighth house is vacant.
2. If Venus and Jupiter are posited in the Ninth house, Mercury in the ascendant and Mars in the Seventh house.
3. If the ascendant lord, Eighth lord, Tenth lord and Saturn all are strong.
4. If the ascendant lord is posited in the ascendant and the Eighth lord in the Eighth house.
5. If the Eighth lord or Saturn is conjunct an exalted planet.
6. If the Moon is exalted and conjunct Jupiter and Mars.
7. If there are no malefic planets in square houses and Jupiter is placed in a square position (1,4,7,10) as counted from the ascendant lord.

8. In a chart of Cancer or Taurus ascendant, if Jupiter is placed in the ascendant and three more planets are exalted.

9. If in a chart of Cancer ascendant, Jupiter is posited in the ascendant and at least two planets are exalted.

10. If the ascendant lord is strong and any three planets are placed in their own signs or their *mooltrikona* signs.

11. If Jupiter is posited in the Eighth house and the Moon in the Eleventh and the ascendant lord is exalted.

12. If all the planets including strong Moon are posited in odd signs.

13. If strong and affliction-free benefic planets are posited in the Sixth or Eighth houses.

14. If the ascendant lord is conjunct a trine lord.

15. If the ascendant lord is exceptionally strong and is posited in a square house and it is aspected by only benefic planets. This combination is known as *navesh* yoga and confers long life and good luck.

Yogas indicating widowhood

1. Rahu posited in the Second house and Mars in the Seventh house.

2. If the ascendant lord and Seventh lord both are placed in the Eighth house.

3. If the Seventh lord falls in inimical or debilitation sign and it is conjunct or aspected by malefic planet.

4. If the Seventh lord is in inimical or debilitation sign and aspected by malefic planet and the Seventh house is under malefic influence.

5. If the Seventh lord, Second lord or Venus are conjunct malefic planets and are also receiving malefic aspects.
6. If the Seventh lord is posited in the Eighth house and the Twelfth lord is in the Seventh house.
7. If Venus is posited in the Eighth house and Eighth lord in the Seventh house.
8. The Moon placed in the Sixth or Eighth house.
9. If the Seventh or Eighth houses from the ascendant or the Moon are occupied by malefic planets.
10. If the Second house and its lord both receive aspects from Jupiter and Mars.

Example 2.1: The longevity analysis of the chart of a male native who died at the age of seventy-eight years.

Date of Birth: 23 November 1902
Place of birth: 72 E 40, 23 N 06
Time of birth: 05:16:00 LMT
Dasha balance at birth: Venus: Sixteen years, One month, Eight days

Table 2.2: Planetary data for the birth chart 2.1

Planet/ Asc	Sign	Longi- tude	Constellation	Constella- tion lord
Asc	Libra	22:47	*Vishakha*	Ju
Su	Scorpio	07:17	*Anuradha*	Sa
Mo	Leo	15:57	*Poorvaphalguni*	Ve
Ma	Leo	24:11	*Poorvaphalguni*	Ve

Me	Libra	26:24	Vishakha	Ju
Ju	Capricorn	18:43	Shravan	Mo
Ve	Scorpio	05:47	Anuradha	Sa
Sa	Capricorn	01:17	Utraashadha	Su
Ra	Libra	00:44	Chitra	Ma
Ke	Aries	00:44	Ashvini	Ke

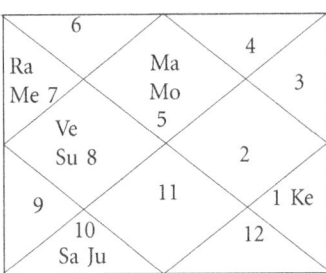

Chart 2.1: Birth chart

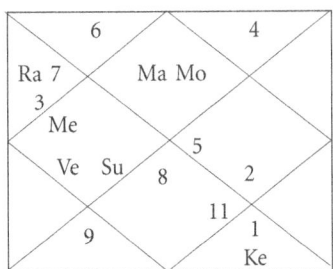

Chart 2.2: Moon chart for the birth chart 2.1

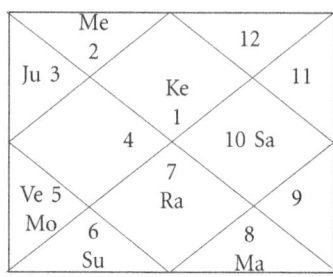

Chart 2.3: Navamsha chart for the birth chart 2.1

Analysis of the charts for longevity

First of all we estimate the lifespan category as per the method discussed earlier in this chapter:

1. (a) Ascendant lord   (b) Eighth lord
2. (a) Ascendant   (b) Moon
3. (a) Moon   (b) Saturn

Observing the signs of the above constituents from the birth chart 2.1 we get as below:

4. (a) Scorpio   (b) Scorpio
5. (a) Libra   (b) Leo
6. (a) Leo   (b) Capricorn

Interpreting these signs in terms of the lifespan categories as given in the table 2.1 we get as below:

4. Alp aayu
5. Madhyam aayu
6. Madhyam aayu

Therefore, the lifespan category indicated is madhyam aayu that between thirty-two to seventy-five years.

To analyse the charts for longevity

In the Birth chart 2.1 the Eighth lord Venus is also the ascendant lord and it is posited in the Second house with the Eleventh lord Sun and aspects the Eighth house. The Eighth lord is in the constellation of *yogakaraka* planet Saturn. Saturn, the significator of longevity, is a *yogakarak* and posited in its own sign. Also it is a *vargotam* planet.

With respect to the Moon, the Eighth lord is Jupiter and it is conjunct Saturn the significator of longevity, also Saturn aspects the Eighth house. As per the Moon sign, Mars is a yogakarak planet and it aspects the Eighth house, Mars is in the constellation of Venus. In the navamsha chart, Mars is posited in its own sign. Moon is also a vargotam planet.

From the above analysis, long lifespan is indicated; hence the native died at the age of seventy-eight years. The death occurred during the antardasha of Mercury in the main *dasha* of Saturn, both these planets are maraka grehas as per the Moon chart 2.2

Example 2.3: The longevity analysis of the chart of a male native who lived for thirty-nine years.

Date of Birth: 25 December 1917
Place of birth: 00 W 05, 51 N 31
Time of birth: 23:55:00 GMT
Dasha balance at birth: Moon: Eight years, Eight month, Twenty-six days

Table 2.3: Planetary data for the Birth chart 2.4

Planet/ Asc	Sign	Longi- tude	Constellation	Constella- tion lord
Asc	Virgo	09:06	*Utraphalguni*	Su
Su	Sagittarius	10:56	*Moola*	Ke
Mo	Taurus	11:42	*Rohini*	Mo
Ma	Virgo	02:19	*Utraphalguni*	Su
Me	Sagittarius	26:56	*Utraashadha*	Su
Ju	Taurus	10:24	*Rohini*	Mo
Ve	Capricorn	25:09	*Dhanishtha*	Ma
Sa	Cancer	21:01	*Ashlesha*	Me
Ra	Sagittarius	08:38	*Moola*	Ke
Ke	Gemini	08:38	*Ardra*	Ra

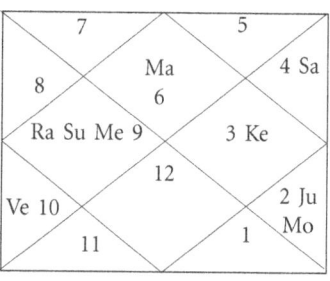

Chart 2.4: Birth chart

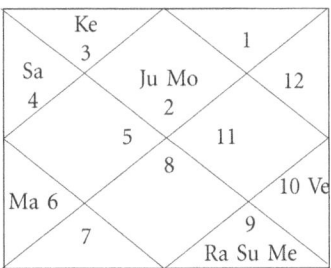

Chart 2.5: Moon chart for the birth chart 2.4

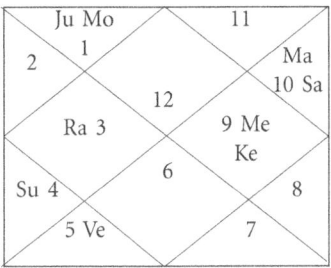

Chart 2.6: Navamsha chart for the birth chart 2.4

Analysis of charts for longevity

In the Birth chart 2.4 the Eighth house is aspected by the Mars, Sixth lord Saturn and debilitated Rahu. The Eighth lord Mars is posited in inimical sign at the Sixth place from the Eighth house and it is aspected by the Sixth lord Saturn. The Eighth lord Mars is aspected by Jupiter, which is death-inflicting planet (marak) because it is the Second lord. Saturn, which signifies longevity, is posited in an inimical sign.

As per the Moon chart 2.5, the Eighth house is occupied by debilitated Rahu and afflicted Mercury. The house is aspected by the Twelfth lord Mars and debilitated Ketu. The Eighth lord of the Moon chart is Jupiter and it is placed at the Sixth place from the Eighth house in an inimical sign. In this chart, the significator Saturn is posited at the Eighth place from the Eighth house.

In the navamsha chart 2.6 Rahu and Ketu and the Eighth lord Mars become exalted also the Eighth lord of the navamsha chart, viz., Venus is aspected by ascendant lord Jupiter. Because of these positive effects, the native entered the madhyam aayu category and lived up to thirty-nine years in spite of heavy afflictions of birth and Moon charts. Death occurred in the antardasha of Mercury in the dasha of Jupiter. Jupiter, as we have mentioned above, is the marak planet for this native and Mercury is a heavily afflicted one.

3

PLANETS AND DISEASES

The planets influence every aspect of human life. All students and experts of Vedic or Hindu astrology know that there are seven planets, which have physical existence and these are the Sun, Moon, Mars, Mercury, Jupiter, Venus, and Saturn. But there are two strategic hypothetical points on the ecliptic which are also treated as planets and these are Rahu and Ketu or respectively the North and South nodes of the Moon.

From the astronomical view, the Sun is not a planet and is rather a star; but mainly because of its powerful radiation and magnetic influences on the Earth we consider it as a planet. Also the Moon irrespective of it being just a satellite of the Earth, is considered a planet mainly because of its strong gravitational pull due to its close proximity to the Earth.

Each planet signifies a lot of things but here in this book, we shall consider the body parts or functions and diseases represented by each of the above-mentioned nine planets. The body parts, elements and body humours represented by each planet are given in the following tables 3.1 to 3.3 respectively.

Table 3.1: The body parts as represented by each planet.

Planet	Body part or function and constituents it represents
Sun	Heart, stomach, head, right-eye, bones, general constitution of the body
Moon	Blood, body-fluids, lungs, mind, left-eye, breast
Mars	Red blood corpuscles, marrow, genitals, rectum, head, veins and vitality
Mercury	Chest, nerves, skin, naval, spinal system
Jupiter	Thighs, fat, liver, ear, memory and spleen
Venus	Face, vision, genitals, touch, semen, body-lustre and throat
Saturn	Legs, teeth, arteries and hair
Rahu	Feet, neck, breathing
Ketu	Stomach, feet

Table 3.2: The elements represented by each planet

Planet	Element or tatva it represents
Sun	Fire
Moon	Water
Mars	Fire
Mercury	Earth

Jupiter	Aakash (a subtle non-physical element)
Venus	Water
Saturn	Air

Table 3.3: The body humours as represented by each planet.

Planet	Body humour or *dosha* it represents
Sun	*Pit*
Moon	*Vaat and kafa*
Mars	*Pit*
Mercury	*Vaat, pit and kafa*
Jupiter	*Kafa*
Venus	*Vaat and kafa*
Saturn	*Vaat*

We shall now describe each of these planets from medical point of view in order to know their elemental nature, the humour they represent and probable diseases each can cause when under affliction or weak and malefic condition in a chart.

SUN

The Sun represents the fire element and the pit dosha (humour) in the body. Sun is the significator for health, vitality, body strength and dynamism. If the Sun is posited in the ascendant it gives baldness, short temper and aggressive or bossy behaviour.

If under affliction or in a position to give disease, it can cause heart diseases, stomach troubles, digestive problems such as indigestion, eyesight problems particularly in the right eye, wear and tear of the skin, bone fractures and serious ailments because of accumulated toxins in the body.

MOON

It represents the water element and kafa dosha in the body. It is the *karaka* (significator) for mind, left-eye, body fluids, breast, etc. One may feel anxiety, discontentment and low in spirits because of weak Moon in the chart.

Under affliction or in a position to give disease, it can cause emotional imbalance, insomnia, pleurisy, tuberculoses, dropsy, respiratory problems, chest complaints, disturbed menstrual flow in women, breast cancer, vomiting and diarrhoea, cold and fever and mental problems.

MARS

It represents the fire element and the pit dosha in the body. It is the significator for muscular power, head, marrow, red blood corpuscles, energy, confidence, sexual vitality, etc.

If it is in a position to give disease, then it can cause blood-related ailments, cuts and boils, fever, accidents, excessive body heat and related problems, itching, piles and diseases of reproductive organs including the uterus. Mars along with the Moon can cause menstrual irregularities and related troubles in women.

MERCURY

It represents the Earth element and all the three dosha-s (humours), viz., vaat, pit and kafa in the body. Mercury is the significator for skin, nerves, intellect, speech, etc. If it is a disease-giving planet in the chart, then it can cause speech and hearing disorders, skin diseases, nervous troubles and ailments of ear and nose.

JUPITER

It represents the aakash element. The nearest equivalent to aakash in English language is ether but this word is not adequate to represent the subtle element, which Jupiter represents. English is a commercial language and not meant to describe the advanced fine sciences of the east. As regards the body humours Jupiter represents the kafa dosha.

Jupiter stands for liver, gall bladder, spleen, body-fat and pancreas. It can cause diabetes, ear troubles, fever, unconsciousness and long-term diseases. If under affliction it makes one lethargic.

VENUS

It represents the water element and vaat and kafa humours in the body.

It stands for vision, urine, semen, etc. Under affliction, it can cause sex and urine-related problems, poor vision, carbuncle, typhoid and appendicitis.

SATURN

It represents the vaat humour and air element in the body. It stands for legs, feet, nerves, glandular secretions, etc. If it is a disease-causing planet in a chart, then it can cause complicated and long-term diseases and sometimes diseases, which are not easily diagnosed. It can cause tumours, cancer, nervous weakness, stomach ailments, wind troubles, paralysis and ailments related to feet.

RAHU

Rahu behaves like the planet Saturn so it can cause all troubles caused by Saturn and in addition to these, it can cause weakness, heart diseases, leprosy, clouded mentality and fear of the unknown, cancer, epilepsy, chicken pox, dental problems, snake bite and injuries due to animals. Rahu mainly influences the brain and blood. It can also give suicidal tendencies.

If Rahu is a benefic and in a strong position in the chart, then it gives mobility, health, dynamism and good level of awareness to the native.

KETU

Ketu behaves like the planet Mars; hence all ailments represented by Mars can be caused also by Ketu. In addition to these it can cause chicken and small pox, viral fevers, intestinal worms and problems of feet and anus.

Ketu mainly influences the blood and skin. If Ketu in a chart is strong and benefic, then the native is bold, energetic, enthusiastic and active. Also it gives recuperative powers and resistance to diseases.

4

SIGNS AND DISEASES

The zodiac which is an imaginary belt in the heavens all around the earth is divided into twelve equal parts of thirty degrees each and these are termed as signs or *rashi*-s. Each sign has some unique characteristics. In Vedic or Hindu astrology, the sign falling in the ascendant in the birth chart and the Moon sign or the sign in which the natal Moon falls, carry special importance and define the general characteristics of the native.

We give below the essential details for medical diagnosis for each of the twelve signs. These include the planets, which are the lords of the signs, the elements, body parts and diseases represented by the signs and the general characteristics. The general characteristics apply only to the ascendant sign and to the Moon sign in a birth chart.

ARIES

Lord Planet: Mars

Elemental nature: Fire

Body parts it rules: Head, brain and pineal gland.

Diseases it represents: Headache, migraine, head cold, fever, haemorrhage, high blood pressure, body pain, poor self-confidence, weakness, mental problems, scalp and hair-related troubles, such as dandruff and premature greying, meningitis and insomnia.

General characteristics: Generally the native has good immunity and resistance to diseases particularly to infectious diseases. But the body is prone to injuries and dangers of accidents. Must avoid stimulants and meat in excess.

TAURUS

Lord Planet: Venus

Elemental nature: Earth

Body parts it rules: Eyes, Face, Mouth, Teeth and Tonsils

Diseases it represents: Pimples on face and eruptions in the mouth, speech disorders, eye sight or vision problems, loss of facial beauty, gum troubles, blocked nose, dental troubles and ENT problems.

General characteristics: Normally the body is robust and strong, but if it falls ill then the recovery is slow. This fact necessitates care. One should take medical help if the symptoms prolong.

GEMINI

Lord Planet: Mercury

Elemental nature: Air

Body parts it rules: Arms, hands, fingers, shoulders, upper ribs, lungs, bronchial tract, thymus gland, nerves and nervous system and collar bone.

Diseases it represents: Nervous system problems, restlessness of mind, chest and lungs complaints, asthma, pleurisy and insomnia.

General characteristics: The main threat to health is from the effects of anxiety and mental strain. Take good sleep and relax occasionally. Also take care of the lungs.

CANCER

Lord Planet: Moon

Elemental nature: Water

Body parts it rules: Breasts, heart, alimentary canal, lower ribs, womb, pancreas, arteries and veins and capillaries.

Diseases it represents: Stomach upsets, poor digestion, breast-related problems including breast cancer, heart diseases, depressed feeling, blood circulation problems, palpitation of heart and respiratory disorders.

General characteristics: Health is generally fragile. The native should take good care of the chest and stomach and must avoid alcoholic drinks.

LEO

Lord Planet: Sun

Elemental nature: Fire

Body parts it rules: Heart, intestines, liver, spleen, kidney and naval.

Diseases it represents: Stomach upsets such as indigestion, gastric troubles, diabetes and heart diseases.

General characteristics: Generally the native enjoys good health and if illness comes, then recovery is quick. They must avoid drinks and stimulants and should have a balanced diet.

VIRGO

Lord Planet: Mercury

Elemental nature: Earth

Body parts it rules: Lower dorsal nerves, bowels and the back.

Diseases it represents: Disorders of bowels and intestines, hernia, backache and problems related to the spinal cord.

General characteristics: In general, the native enjoys good health. Being very active particularly in the young age, the Virgos appear younger than their actual age.

LIBRA

Lord Planet: Venus

Elemental nature: Air

Body parts it rules: Buttocks, uterus.

Diseases it represents: Blight's disease, urinary ailments, nephrites, lumbago, and venereal diseases.

General characteristics: The Libra-born native lacks immunity against infectious diseases. So, they must take great care.

SCORPIO

Lord Planet: Mars

Elemental nature: Fire

Body parts it rules: Genitals, anus, pelvic bone, and vertebral column.

Diseases it represents: Piles, ailments of reproductive and excretory systems.

General characteristics: Here, Moon being the lord of the house of obstructions, can cause ill health; so a Scorpio-born needs to keep a cool mind.

SAGITTARIUS

Lord Planet: Jupiter

Elemental nature: Fire

Body parts it rules: Liver, hips, femur, muscles, thighs, thighbone and pelvis.

Diseases it represents: Weakness of hips and thigh muscles, sciatica, swellings, overweight and resulting problems.

General characteristics: Native born in this sign needs to be moderate and keep the mind in balance. The more freedom you have, the better you feel.

CAPRICORN

Lord Planet: Saturn

Elemental nature: Earth

Body parts it rules: Bones, joints, teeth and knees.

Diseases it represents: Pain in knees, weakness of knee muscles, arthritis, dental problems, poor growth and skin problems.

General characteristics: Great care is needed to see that the native born in this sign does not get depressed and discontented. Also the digestive system is vulnerable for those born in this sign.

AQUARIUS:

Lord Planet: Saturn

Elemental nature: Air

Body parts it rules: Ankles, circulatory system, calves and shins.

Diseases it represents: Circulatory problems, varicose veins, anxiety, arthritis and palpitation.

General characteristics: Native born in this sign is susceptible to infectious diseases. He/She needs to take lot of rest and avoid overtaxing the body.

PISCES

Lord Planet: Jupiter

Elemental nature: Water

Body parts it rules: Feet (from heals to toes).

Diseases it represents: Swelling of feet, cracks in heals, immune system problems, hormonal imbalance and glandular problems.

General characteristics: For native born in this sign, alcoholic drinks are harmful. He/She needs to take care to avoid gastric troubles in particular.

Classification of signs

Like the various classifications of houses or *bhavas*, the signs are also classified in various groups. One of the classifications is based on the elemental nature of signs and is useful in medical astrology; the same is given below in the Table 4.1.

Table 4.1: Signs and the elements they represent

Element	Signs representing it
Fire	Aries, Leo and Sagittarius
Earth	Taurus, Virgo and Capricorn
Air	Gemini, Libra and Aquarius
Water	Cancer, Scorpio and Pisces

Characteristics of these elements:

Fiery signs

The fiery signs denote vigour, vitality, energy, self-confidence, self-reliance and enthusiasm. The native has tendency to sudden illness, which normally do not last long. They are prone to fevers, inflammations, boils, bilious troubles etc.

Earthy signs

These signs indicate stability, firmness and general good health. If the native falls ill, then comparatively longer time is needed for recovery. Their main troubles are from restlessness, anxiety and chronic disorders.

Airy signs

Airy signs are connected with the mind, intellect and the nervous system. The native has good circulation system and a plump body. There is tendency to overexert physically as well as mentally, which exhausts their energy; and chances of nervous strain and breakdown are also present.

Watery signs

The native with watery sign has poor recuperative power. So if such a native falls ill, then chances of illness getting prolonged are very much there. They have generally weak constitution and poor reserves of energy. They have a sensitive mind. Main perils are anaemia, tumours, cancer and lack of stamina. Also troubles related to digestion, urine and catarrh could occur.

5

HOUSES AND DISEASES

The whole life of a native is contained in the twelve houses called bhavas of a birth chart. Apart from other significations each house also signifies a particular body part. In fact, these body parts are as per the Kaalpurush Kundali or the chart of the time personified which is simply the chart of Aries ascendant sign as shown in Fig. 5.1.

Incidentally, let me remark here that the deep thought and concepts laid down by our ancient sages have inspired the western scientists. Albert Einstein in his theory of relativity, which got him the Nobel prize, considered time as a dimension but the fact that our wise sages went a step ahead and even personified time did not get open recognition from western scientists.

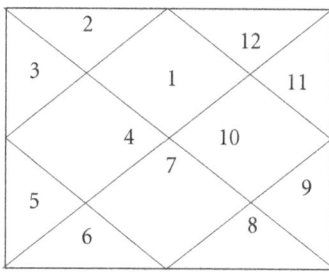

Fig. 5.1: Kaalpurush Kundali

The various body parts corresponding to this chart are shown in the Table 5.1 below.

Table 5.1: Houses and the body parts they represent as per the Kaalpurush Kundali

House	Body part it represents
1st	Head (above eyes)
2nd	Right eye, face up to chin
3rd	Arms, right hand, neck, ears, breast, throat
4th	Heart, lungs, chest
5th	Stomach
6th	Back
7th	Genitals
8th	Anus, hips
9th	Thighs
10th	Knees
11th	Calf, left hand
12th	Feet, toes, left eye

Classifications of houses

There are various classifications of the houses of a chart. One classification is as per the elements represented by the houses as shown in the Table 5.2.

Table 5.2: Classification of houses as per elements

Element	Houses it represents
Fire	1,5,9
Earth	2,6,10
Air	3,7,11
Water	4,8,12

Another classification is shown in the Table 5.3.

Table 5.3: Another classification of houses

Houses	Classification
1,4,7,10	Square, cardinal or angular houses
2,5,8,11	Succedent houses
3,6,9,12	Cadent houses

Diseases and houses

As per medical astrology, the principles of each house denotes some common diseases, which can occur because of the involvement of that house. Some common diseases for all the twelve houses are listed in the Table 5.4.

Table 5.4: Diseases represented by houses

House	Diseases it represents
1st	Brain tumour, brain cancer, headache, insanity, weak memory, epilepsy, brain haemorrhage and going into coma.
2nd	Eye troubles especially in the right eye, throat, tongue and teeth troubles and speech disorders.
3rd	Ear problem, ailments of arms, shoulders and right hand.
4th	Heart and lung diseases and chest complaints.
5th	Liver and stomach ailments, diarrhoea, heart disease, viral disease and diseases of the intestines.
6th	Bachache and related problems, problems related to large intestine, diabetes, ulcers, colic and appendicitis.
7th	Ailments related to the urinal system, kidneys, uterus, ovaries, testicles and prostrate gland.
8th	Diseases of genitals and rectum, piles, fistula and ulcers.
9th	Excessive fat on hips and thighs and problems caused by this, and paralysis.
10th	Knee troubles, like pain and loss of mobility.
11th	Ailments of legs, left ear and calf.
12th	Problems related to feet and left eye and insomnia.

The Table 5.5 below describes the diseases caused due to imbalance of various elements.

Table 5.5: Diseases resulting due to imbalance of elements tatvas in the body.

Element or tatva	Type of disease due to its imbalance
Fire *(Agni)*	Fevers, boils and pimples, eyesight problems, jaundice, blood problems and weakness.
Air *(Vayu)*	Ailments of joints, arthritis, inflammation, wind troubles in the stomach, body pain and stiffness of neck.
Water *(Jal)*	Respiratory and lung-related problems, pneumonia, typhoid, cancer, tuberculosis, cough and colds, vomiting, diarrhoea, troubles related to urine, semen and blood.
Earth *(Bhumi)*	Marrow, muscles, skin and hair diseases, pain inflammation, disproportionate body parts and disability.
Element or tatva	**Type of disease due to its imbalance.**
Aakash*	Unconsciousness, problems arising due to strong feelings of love, attachments, anger and opposition.

*Note: The Sanskrit and Hindi word aakash represents the subtle element for which the English language does not have a proper word. Some authors use the word ether but that is not adequate.

Death-inflicting houses

The Second and Seventh houses in a chart are called marak sthanas or the death-inflicting houses. The logic behind this is explained below.

The Eighth house in the birth chart represents longevity or the span of life. According to the principle of *Bhavaat bhavam niyaye* the Eighth from the Eighth house, viz., the Third house also represents the longevity of the native. In fact, the above principle states that whatever a house at certain number of places from the ascendant signifies, the house at same number of places from that house signifies the same significations.

We also know that the Twelfth house to any house is considered the house of loss to that house. Therefore, the Second and Seventh which are the Twelfth for Third and Eighth houses respectively, represent the houses of loss of longevity or in other words the houses of death or marak sthanas. Planets related to these maraka houses during their periods can either give death or suffering due to diseases, etc.

The house of obstructions

In every birth chart there is a house of obstructions also called the *badhak sthana*. This house is determined as per the ascendant sign from the Table 5.6:

Table 5.6: The house of obstruction and the obstructionist planet for birth charts of different ascendant signs

The ascendant sign	The house of obstruction	The obstructionist planet
Aries, Cancer, Libra, Capricorn	11th house	Saturn, Venus, Sun, Mars respectively
Taurus, Leo, Scorpio, Aquarius	9th house	Saturn, Mars, Moon, Venus respectively
Gemini, Virgo, Sagittarius, Pisces	7th house	Jupiter, Mercury respectively

The house of obstruction and its lord can cause health-related problems in particular.

6

CONSTELLATIONS AND DISEASES

The earth revolves around the Sun along an elliptical path, which in astronomy is called the ecliptic. We assume an imaginary belt extending about 8º North and 8º South of the ecliptic, which means it is about 16º wide. This imaginary belt is called the zodiac, in which all the planets revolve in their respective orbits.

The zodiac is divided into twelve equal parts of 30º each called the signs. There is considered another division of the zodiac into twenty-seven equal parts of 13º:20' each and these are known as constellations or Nakshatras or lunar mansions. Each sign occupies two and a quarter constellations.

As there are nine planets, a group of three constellations fall under the lordship of each planet. Because a constellation is a part of a sign, therefore, it is under the influence of two planets, viz., the sign lord and the constellation lord.

The constellation of the ascendant and that of the natal Moon, both play an important role in the life of the native, the indications given below as general characteristics and the medical indications are based on these constellations. Some astrologers give more importance to the constellation of the strongest between the ascendant and the natal Moon (the author supports this view).

The general and medical indications for each of the twenty-seven constellations are described below:

1. *Ashvini*:

Location: 00º:00' to 13º:20' Aries

Sign lord: Mars

Constellation lord: The South node (Ketu)

General characteristics: The native is clever, intelligent, lucky, honest, efficient, short-tempered and popular.

Medical indications: The native is vulnerable to fever, windy troubles, clouded mentality, insomnia, mental disturbances and pain, Alzheimer's disease, epilepsy and headaches.

2. *Bharni*:

Location: 13º:20' to 26º:40' Aries

Sign lord: Mars

Constellation lord: Venus

General characteristics: The native is pleasure seeking, aspiring, truthful, clever, determined, courageous but selfish and indulgent.

Medical indications: Cold, trembling due to cold, fever, body pain, weakness, lethargy and low level of efficiency are represented by this constellation.

3(A). *Kritika* (The 1st quarter falling in Aries sign):

Location: 26°:40' to 30°:00' Aries

Sign lord: Mars

Constellation lord: Sun

General characteristics: The native is enthusiastic, competitive, go-getter type and has leadership qualities.

Medical indications: Pain in the eyes, excessive body heat, disturbed sleep, pain in the knees, heart trouble, cerebral meningitis, brain fever, injury, accidents and danger of fire.

3(B). *Kritika* (Remaining three quarters):

Location: 0°:00' to 10°:00' Taurus

Sign lord: Venus

Constellation lord: Sun

General characteristics: The native likes company of others and is sociable, generous, courteous and pleasure seeking.

Medical indications: Pimples on face, stiffness of neck, tonsils, pain in lower jaw and ailments of larynx.

4 *Rohini:*

Location: 10°:00' to 23°:20' Taurus

Sign lord: Venus

Constellation lord: Moon

General characteristics: The native is cordial, well-mannered, sympathetic, truthful and good-looking.

Medical indications: Fever, pain in ribs, cervical problems, apoplexy, breast pain, swelling, sore throat, cold and cough.

5(A). *Mrigshira* (first two quarters):

Location: 23°:20' to 30°:00' Taurus

Sign lord: Venus

Constellation lord: Mars

General characteristics: The native is alert and aware, witty, strong, enthusiastic, attractive, selfish and quarrelsome.

Medical indications: Cold and cough, tonsils, problems of chin and face, pimples, throat pain, diphtheria and venereal distemper.

5(B). *Mrigshira* (last two quarters):

Location: 0º:00' to 6º:40' Gemini

Sign lord: Mercury

Constellation lord: Mars

General characteristics: The native is witty, sharp, quick to react, impulsive, easily excitable, timid and passionate.

Medical indications: Goitre, skin diseases, speech disorders, problems of arms, shoulders and upper ribs.

6. *Ardra:*

Location: 6º:40' to 20º:00' Gemini

Sign lord: Mercury

Constellation lord: The North node (Rahu)

General characteristics: The native is ingenious, perceptive, resourceful and mentally active.

Medical indications: Problems of throat, arms and shoulders, septic throat, mumps, asthma, dry cough, ear-troubles, pain in body and confused mind.

7(A). *Punarvasu* (first three quarters):

Location: 20º:00' to 30º:00' Gemini

Sign lord: Mercury

Constellation lord: Jupiter

General characteristics: The native is intuitive, good-looking and has broad mind, good memory, wisdom and a balanced mind.

Medical indications: Ear, throat, shoulders, lungs, chest and respiratory system problems, pain in chest.

7(B). *Punarvasu* (fourth quarter):

Location: 0º:00' to 3º:20' Cancer
Sign lord: Moon
Constellation lord: Jupiter
General characteristics: The native has good imagination and judgment and is benevolent, compassionate and sympathetic.
Medical indications: Stomach problems, ailments of diaphragm, pancreas and liver. Excessive fat on chest.

8. *Pushya:*

Location: 3º:20' to 16º:40' Cancer
Sign lord: Moon
Constellation lord: Saturn

General characteristics: The native is mentally composed, careful, patient and learned.
Medical indications: Tuberculosis, gallstone, cough, cancer, jaundice, eczema and dyspepsia.

9. *Ashlesha:*

Location: 16º:40' to 30º:00' Cancer

Sign lord: Moon

Constellation lord: Mercury

General characteristics: The native has ingenious and sharp mind and likes travelling.

Medical indications: Weak body and tendency to fall ill. Wind in stomach, pain in knees and legs, nervousness, indigestion and breathing difficulties.

10. *Magha:*

Location: 0º:00' to 13º:20' Leo

Sign lord: Sun

Constellation lord: The South node (Ketu)

General characteristics: The native is short-tempered, impulsive, industrious, sensual and outspoken.

Medical indications: Heart trouble, backache, cholera, spinal meningitis, palpitation of heart, kidney stone.

11. *Poorva Phalguni:*

Location: 13º:20' to 26º:40' Leo

Sign lord: Sun

Constellation lord: Venus

General characteristics: The native is generous, affectionate, honest and sweet-tongued person.

Medical indications: Anaemia, pain in legs, heart-valve problems, swelling in ankles.

12 (A). *Utra Phalguni* (first quarter):

Location: 26º: 40' to 30º:00' Leo

Sign lord: Sun

Constellation lord: Sun

General characteristics: The native is optimistic, contented, happy, rich and likes to show of.

Medical indications: Fever, blood pressure problems, blood clotting in brain.

12 (B). *Utra Phalguni* (last three quarters):

Location: 0º:00' to 10º:00' Virgo

Sign lord: Mercury

Constellation lord: Sun

General characteristics: The native is tactful, intelligent, studious and industrious.

Medical indications: Madness, sore throat, spinal cord and intestine problems.

13. *Hasta:*

Location: 10°:00' to 23°:20' Virgo

Sign lord: Mercury

Constellation lord: Moon

General characteristics: The native is industrious, full of energy, quarrelsome and courageous.

Medical indications: Loose motions, excessive gas formation, breathing troubles, hysteria, typhoid, weakness of arms and shoulders.

14(A) *Chitra* (first two quarters):

Location: 23°:20' to 30°:00' Virgo

Sign lord: Mercury

Constellation lord: Mars

General characteristics: The native is practical, courageous, and full of energy, active, restless and irritable.

Medical indications: Brain fever, acute body pain, itching and irritation and headache.

14(B). *Chitra* (last two quarters):

Location: 0°:00' to 6°:40' Libra

Sign lord: Venus

Constellation lord: Mars

General characteristics: The native is adventurous, perceptive and intuitive and loves science.

Medical indications: Excess urine, kidney problems, ulcers, appendicitis and hernia.

15. *Swati:*

Location: 6°:40' to 20°:00' Libra

Sign lord: Venus

Constellation lord: The North node (Rahu)

General characteristics: The native is adaptive, sensitive, initiative peaceful, social and compassionate.

Medical indications: Leprosy, hernia, urinary troubles and eczema.

16 (A). *Vishakha* (**First three quarters**):

Location: 20°:00' to 30°:00' Libra

Sign lord: Venus

Constellation lord: Jupiter

General characteristics: The native is good-mannered, polite, atheist, generous, truthful and just and believes in universal brotherhood and love.

Medical indications: Diseases of womb, dropsy and prostrate enlargement.

16 (B). *Vishakha* (fourth quarter):

Location: 0º:00' to 3º:20' Scorpio

Sign lord: Mars

Constellation lord: Jupiter

General characteristics: The native is straight-forward, sincere, independent, generous, wise and has a longer lifespan.

Medical indications: Nose bleeding, renal stone, menstrual troubles and tumours.

17. *Anuradha:*

Location: 3º:20' to 16º:40' Scorpio

Sign lord: Mars

Constellation lord: Saturn

General characteristics: The native is self-centred, aggressive, courageous, intelligent, straight-forward and hard working.

Medical indications: Constipation, piles, nasal catarrh, sterility.

18. *Jyeshtha:*

Location: 16º:40' to 30º:00' Scorpio

Sign lord: Mars

Constellation lord: Mercury

General characteristics: The native is spontaneous, learned, practical, philosophical and witty.

Medical indications: Bleeding piles, fistula, bowel infection, leucorrhoea, pain in arms and shoulders.

19. *Moola:*

Location: 0°:00' to 13°:20' Sagittarius

Sign lord: Jupiter

Constellation lord: The South node (Ketu)

General characteristics: The native is aggressive, grave-looking, proud, generous, cordial, charitable, honest and law-abiding.

Medical indications: Rheumatism, low blood pressure, cold feet and hands.

20. *Poorva ashadha:*

Location: 13°:20' to 26°:40' Sagittarius

Sign lord: Jupiter

Constellation lord: Venus

General characteristics: The native is broad-minded, polite, compassionate, hopeful, extravagant, sensitive to other's feelings and honest.

Medical indications: Diabetes, lung cancer, headache and body pain.

21 (A). *Utra ashadha* (first quarter):

Location: 26°:40' to 30°:00' Sagittarius

Sign lord: Jupiter

Constellation lord: Sun

General characteristics: The native is righteous-living, charitable, good-natured, fur-loving, successful in religious activities.

Medical indications: Eczema, leprosy pain.

21 (B). *Utra ashadha* (Last three quarters):

Location: 0°:00' to 10°:00' Capricorn

Sign lord: Saturn

Constellation lord: Sun

General characteristics: The native is well-organised, sincere, reliable, intelligent, foresighted and thrifty.

Medical indications: Palpitation of heart, cardiac thrombosis, boils and gastric troubles in stomach.

22. *Shravan:*

Location: 10°:00' to 2°:20' Capricorn

Sign lord: Saturn

Constellation lord: Moon

General characteristics: The native is pessimistic, extra cautious, thrifty and timid.

Medical indications: Skin diseases, tuberculosis, pleurisy and poor digestion.

23 (A). *Dhanishtha* (first two quarters):

Location: 23°:20' to 30°:00' Capricorn

Sign lord: Saturn

Constellation lord: Mars

General characteristics: The native is active, strong-willed, careful, selfish and greedy.

Medical indications: Malaria, high fever, boils and dry cough.

23 (B). *Dhanishtha* (Last two quarters):

Location: 0°:00' to 6°:40' Aquarius

Sign lord: Saturn

Constellation lord: Mars

General characteristics: The native is short-tempered, reliable, social, charitable and logical.

Medical indications: Leg injury, high blood pressure, insomnia, fainting.

24. *Shatbhisha:*

Location: 6°:40' to 20°:00' Aquarius

Sign lord: Saturn

Constellation lord: The North node (Rahu)

General characteristics: The native is independent, patient, and leisure-loving and lazy.

Medical indications: High blood pressure, palpitation of heart, insomnia, amputation, leprosy, eczema, rheumatism.

25 (A). *Poorva Bhadrapad* (first three quarters):

Location: 20°:00' to 30°:00' Aquarius

Sign lord: Saturn

Constellation lord: Jupiter

General characteristics: The native is optimistic, honest, reliable and able to take work from others.

Medical indications: Circulatory system problems, swelling of feet, jaundice and abdominal tumour.

25 (B). *Poorva Bhadrapad* (the last quarter):

Location: 0°:00' to 3°:20' Pisces

Sign lord: Jupiter

Constellation lord: Jupiter

General characteristics: The native is music and art lover, polite, broad-minded and joyful.

Medical indications: Enlarged liver, hernia and corn in feet.

26. Utra Bhadrapad:

Location: 3º:20' to 16º:40' Pisces

Sign lord: Jupiter

Constellation lord: Saturn

General characteristics: The native is philosophical, peace and seclusion-loving, helpful and independent.

Medical indications: Hernia, foot fracture, constipation, indigestion, cold feet and tuberculosis.

27. *Revati:*

Location: 16º:40' to 30º:00' Pisces

Sign lord: Jupiter

Constellation lord: Mercury

General characteristics: The native is intuitive, sympathetic, clever, honest, studious and flexible.

Medical indications: Intestinal ulcers, deafness, pus in ear, abdominal disorders and mental problems.

7

THE ASCENDANT

The first house called the ascendant is in the true sense the crown of the birth chart. The ascendant sign and its longitude are determined by the sign rising in the eastern horizon at the place and time of birth of a native. The signs in the rest of the eleven houses of the birth chart follow the ascendant sign.

Significations

The ascendant signifies the physical stature, complexion, constitution, character and temperament, vitality, vigour, tendencies, struggle for life, initiative, perseverance, general well-being, determination and courage, etc.

The most auspicious of all the houses

The auspiciousness of the ascendant is manifold. Firstly it is a square or angular house, and we know that the square houses are auspicious and form the core of the birth chart. Secondly it is also a trine house. The three trine houses, viz., First, Fifth and Ninth are also the auspicious houses. So imagine the auspiciousness of the ascendant, as it is a square as well as a trine house.

There is a classification of houses based on the four aspects of human life, viz., Dharma (religion), *Arth* (wealth), *Kaam* (desires) and *Moksha* (emancipation from the compulsory life death cycles). The Table 7.1 below shows this classification.

Table 7.1: Classification of houses as per the aspects of human life

Houses	Classification
1,5,9	Dharma
2,6,10	Arth
3,7,11	Kaam
4,8,12	Moksha

Each of the four aspects stands on a tripod of three houses. We know that unless we follow religion or dharma we cannot live a righteous life. Let us clarify here that the word religion as used here, does not refer to any of the organised religions, like Hinduism, Sikhism, Islam or Christianity; rather it stands for the universal principles of civilised and righteous living with the motto, 'Live and let others live'.

Dharma is of the utmost importance and we may conclude that life progresses based on the tripod of First, Fifth and Ninth houses of dharma. This concept puts the ascendant in the top most priority.

On the mundane plane, the ascendant signifies the most important part of human anatomy as it houses the brain which is not only the Central Processing Unit (CPU) of the complex human computer, but also a relay station between the physical body and the higher self or the soul.

In a particular birth chart, the negative astrological influences or afflictions on the ascendant and its lord can mar the natural auspiciousness of the ascendant and reduce its strength. It is basically the strength and auspiciousness of the ascendant in a chart, which decides about the state of health of our physical and mental being, the self-confidence, self-reliance and the ability to resist disease and recuperate from disease.

The ascendant lord and the planets posited in the ascendant signify a lot in the medical astrology. Because the ascendant signifies the whole body in general, therefore the ascendant lord or the planet placed in the ascendant signifies mainly that body constituent or function which is present in whole or most of the body.

For example, the Sun in general signifies the right eye, heart and bones but when it is either the ascendant lord or it is placed in the ascendant, then it will signify mainly the bones, which are distributed throughout the body.

These significations for all the seven planets are given in the Table 7.2 below.

Table 7.2: Planets and the body part or functions they signify.

Planet	Significations	Significations
	When ascendant lord or posited in the ascendant	When neither the ascendant lord nor posited in the ascendant
Sun	Bones	Right eye, heart, bones
Moon	Blood	Mind, lungs, blood
Mars	Muscles (flesh), red blood corpuscles	Marrow, muscles (flesh), red blood corpuscles
Mercury	Skin	Speech, hearing power and skin
Jupiter	Fat	Stomach, fat, liver
Venus	Blood sugar	Eyesight (vision), urine, semen, blood sugar
Saturn	Nerves	Feet, nerves

Diagnosing diseases

In diagnosing diseases, we need to consider the ascendant lord and the planets placed in the ascendant. If one or more of these are under afflictions, then certain diseases can result during the periods of those planets. The Table 7.3 below shows the probable diseases corresponding to the afflicted planet when the same is either the ascendant lord or placed in the ascendant.

Table 7.3: Diseases resulting from afflicted ascendant lord or the planet posited in the ascendant

Planet as the ascendant lord or placed in the ascendant	Diseases
Sun	Fracture or weakness of bones
Moon	Blood disorders, anaemia
Mars	Beriberi
Mercury	Skin diseases, leprosy, boils
Jupiter	Weakness
Venus	Sex-related problems, diabetes
Saturn	Nervous weakness, paralysis

We need to observe specifically the debilitated ascendant lord in a chart. This means that in a particular chart if the ascendant lord is placed in its sign of debilitation. Under debilitation the lord becomes weak and keeps wrong intentions so taking into consideration the house of its placement the Table 7.4 below lists various diseases, which it can cause to the native of that chart.

Table 7.4: Debilitated ascendant lords and
the relevant diseases

Planet as debilitated ascendant lord	Disease
Sun	Ear troubles
Moon	Dropsy
Mars (Aries ascendant)	Heart and lung diseases
Mars (Scorpio ascendant)	Wounds, sores, ulcers in hips area
Mercury (Gemini ascendant)	Pain in knees
Mercury (Virgo ascendant)	Urinal troubles
Jupiter (Sagittarius ascendant)	Ailments of the mouth
Jupiter (Pisces ascendant)	Ear troubles
Venus (Taurus ascendant)	Stomach disorders
Venus (Libra ascendant)	Eyesight problems
Saturn (Capricorn ascendant)	Heartache
Saturn (Aquarius ascendant)	Respiratory and throat ailments

A planet other than the ascendant lord but associated with the ascendant or its lord or both can cause diseases if that planet is debilitated or combust or very weak in strength. The possible diseases caused by such a planet are given in the Table 7.5 below.

Table 7.5: Probable diseases which a planet can cause when it is either debilitated or combust or weak and associated with the ascendant or its lord or both of these

Debilitated or combust or weak planet other than the ascendant lord but associated with the ascendant or its lord or both of these	Diseases
Sun	Fever, eye-trouble, heart weakness
Moon	Cold and fever, fits, dropsy, excessive phlegm
Mars	Burns, falls, venereal diseases, headache
Mercury	Upsets of body humours, skin diseases, era troubles
Jupiter	Inflammations, pain in feet or buttocks
Venus	Semen or sex-related problems, eye-sight problems, ailments of mouth and urine
Saturn	Pain, wind troubles, nervous troubles

8

THE SIXTH HOUSE

All aspects relating to a person's life are condensed in the twelve houses also called the bhavas of the birth chart.

Each bhava signifies certain matters. It is common among astrologers to address the Sixth bhava as the *Rog* bhava or the house of disease or with slight elaboration as the Rog, Rin and Shatru bhava, viz., the disease, debt and enmity house.

The detailed significations of this house are: enemies and enmity, impediments, disease, disappointments, debt or loan, difficulties, servants and service, conditions of employment, small animals, litigation and all court-related matters, intestines, back, fear of enemies, loss of name, maternal uncle *(mama)*, mother's sister or *mausi,* etc.

Classification of houses

There are some classifications of houses as listed below in Table 8.1 in which the Sixth house also appears.

Table 8.1: Classification of houses, which also include the Sixth house

Name of the house group	Houses involved	Inference
Trik bhavas	Sixth, Eighth and Twelfth	Inauspicious houses
Trishadai bhavas	Third, Sixth and Eleventh	Houses of strength
Upchaya bhavas	Third, Sixth, Tenth and Eleventh	Progressive houses

Is the Sixth house only a negative house?

Although the main house for disease, debt and difficulties is the Sixth house, yet it is wrong to label it as only a negative or inauspicious house. Contrary to the general view about the trik bhavas, the author feels very strongly that this group of houses is very crucial in uplifting a person.

From Table 8.1 we observe that the Sixth house is an integral part of the three groups. Placement of malefic planets including the Sun in the Sixth house gives courage and strength to the native in order to overcome the difficulties and impediments in life.

Placement of Mars, Saturn or Rahu in the Sixth house is observed to give good and favourable results.

If in a chart Jupiter, Venus, Moon and Mercury are posited in the Third, Sixth, Tenth and Eleventh houses respectively a very auspicious combination called *vasumati* yoga is formed and one rises high in life due to this combination. The author emphasises that for this yoga always consider the Third, Sixth, Tenth and Eleventh places with respect to the ascendant only.

Placement of benefic planets in the Sixth, Seventh and Eighth houses is considered good and this combination is known as *lagnadhi* yoga. This yoga makes one learned and also gives wealth, values and high position. A malefic placed in the Sixth house tends to give financial gains. The Sixth house, if occupied by its own lord, gives rise to *harsh* yoga and due to it the native earns name, fame and wealth. These indications are quite adequate to convince that the Sixth house is not just a negative house.

The significators of the Sixth house

There are two significators of this house, viz., Mars and Saturn.

Broadly speaking, accidents, injuries, litigation and court matters, fights, disputes, enmity, theft, etc., fall under Mars whereas disease, difficulties, delays, debts, service matters fall under Saturn.

Disease and the Sixth house

As far as disease is concerned the trik bhavas, viz., the Sixth, Eighth and Twelfth all combined play their role. The Sixth is the main house of disease, the Eighth house being the Third from the Sixth is the strength of disease and thereby due to it the disease may prolong and become complicated and even it may endanger life, as the Eighth is the house of longevity. Because of the involvement of the Twelfth house the patient may require hospitalisation. The Twelfth also stands for loss of money due to expanses involved. Again it is under the jurisdiction of the Twelfth house whether the patient is cured of disease or gets freedom (mukti) in the form of death from the difficulties and suffering due to disease, etc.

Turning point in life

The author believes in a dynamic approach towards some ill-founded beliefs in astrology. It has been observed in some cases that the trik bhavas play a very positive role in the spiritual upliftment of a person.

The difficulties of disease and debt experienced by a person of basically positive attitude may rise through the involvement of the Eighth and Twelfth houses freedom from vice, bad habits and negativities and set one on to the road to spiritual evolution and self-realisation as the ultimate goal of life.

Judging the Sixth house

From the above discussion, it should be clear that the author does not recommend judging the Sixth house alone.

If disease or any other negative aspect is to be judged, then do so from the Sixth, Eighth and Twelfth houses. Similarly, judge the Third, Sixth, and Eleventh houses for gains and judge the progressive opportunities from the Third, Sixth, Tenth and Eleventh houses.

9

LOCATING VULNERABLE PARTS

In this chapter, we look into a set procedure in order to know the most vulnerable areas of a native's body, which are likely to suffer from ailments either from birth or during the periods of relevant planets.

Role of astrological analysis

Let us admit at the outset, that every science has its limitations and the sacred science of astrology is no exception to this rule. Further, astrology could be hundred percent accurate only if everything in life was predestined even to the minute details. We know from experience that there seems to be a certain degree of free will in everyone's life.

This supports the view that all astrological indications are only probabilities, some strong and some weak.

Let us take an example to illustrate the above thought. Suppose in the birth chart of a person, it is indicated that he or she can be a good sportsperson and is not suitable for intellectual pursuits. The same person under parental pressure puts in his or her best efforts and becomes a doctor. Later he finds himself or herself a sort of misfit in this profession and fails to become a good doctor.

It is rare that just by analysing the chart of this person, an astrologer could have predicted that the native will become a doctor simply because the indications are not there. So can you blame the astrologer for this? Yes, had the astrologer been put the question whether or not the native will succeed, as a doctor then a good astrologer would have said no.

Similarly, in case of medical astrology one should get the chart analysed before hand in order to know the vulnerable body parts and probable diseases which one could suffer from. If you are equipped before hand with this information, then either you can steer clear of disease by following astrological remedial measures along with preventive measures or if later some symptoms appear, then you could get rid of the problem before it gets a strong hold.

Astrological analysis should not condition your mind

It is important that astrological analysis doesn't condition you. You may think or some astrologer may scare you that such thing will definitely happen, that is a sort of conditioning and negative use of astrology. Keep a strong mind and believe that timely action can save you in many cases.

The right procedure

First of all, we need to point out the planets, which can possibly cause disease or death.

Try to get a rough estimate of the longevity of the native based upon the information contained in Chapter two of this section. Determine in which category the lifespan falls, viz., balarisht (upto twelve years), alpaayu (upto thirty-two years), madhyam aayu (between thirty-two to sixty-four years) and pooran aayu (beyond sixty-four years). You need to concentrate on the periods of disease causing planets during the lifespan decided above. For knowing all disease-causing planets follow the following points:

1. Take into consideration the death-inflicting planets as described in Chapter two. Periods of these planets in the lifespan predicted are worthy of consideration.

2. List out all malefic planets that are likely to cause diseases and these are: (1) The Sixth, Eighth and Twelfth lords (2) Planets posited in the Sixth house (3) Afflicted weak and debilitated planets related to the ascendant or its lord. (4) Debilitated planets or planets falling in inimical constellations. (5) Malefic planets, which are also, retrograde (6) Lord of the house of obstructions. (7) *Kendraadhipatis* or planets

with lordship of two house when both the houses fall in square *(Kendra)*.

After we figure out the planets, which can cause trouble, we need to locate the most vulnerable organs or areas. For this purpose, the whole body is divided into three parts as shown in Figure 9.1

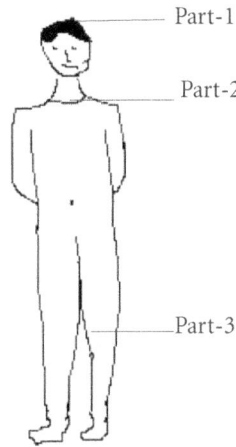

Fig. 9.1: *Division of the body in three parts*

Part 1 is from top of the head to the chin, Part 2 from chin to the naval and Part 3 from naval to the sole of feet. So if we divide a sign into three parts of 10 degree each which is called a *dreshkaan* then the above-mentioned parts fall in three dreshkaans from 0-10º, 10º-20º, 20º-30º respectively. Further, if we make a chart for each of these dreshkaans then the body parts or organs falling in the above-mentioned three divisions are represented by the twelve houses as shown in the following three dreshkaan charts.

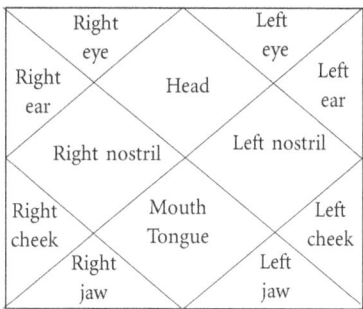

1. Dreshkaan 0–10°

2. Dreshkaan 10°–20°

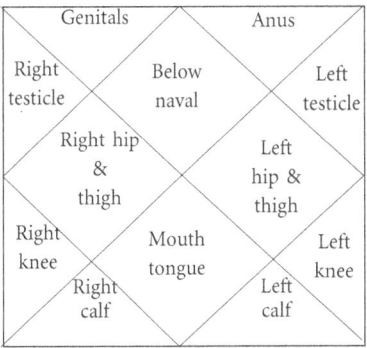

3. Dreshkaan 20º–30º

Now we will explain how to convert a birth chart into a dreshkaan chart. For this purpose use the Table 9.1 as given below.

Table 9.1: Table for converting birth chart to D/3 chart also called a dreshkaan chart

Sign Degree	1	2	3	4	5	6	7	8	9	10	11	12
$0-10^0$	1	4	7	10	1	4	7	10	1	4	7	10
10^0-20^0	2	5	8	11	2	5	8	11	2	5	8	11
20^0-30^0	3	6	9	12	3	6	9	12	3	6	9	12

Note: Numbers 1 to 12 are signs Aries to Pisces.

Now in order to apply the above procedure we consider the birth chart of a native. We will explain how to construct a

D/3 or dreshkaan chart and locate the most vulnerable body areas of this native.

Example 9.1: The birth chart of a heart patient

Date of Birth: 2 July 1941

Place of birth: 77 E 13, 28 N 40

Time of birth: 8:30 AM IST

Dasha **balance at birth (Moon):** Five years, Five months, and Nineteen days

Table 9.2: Planetary data for the Birth chart 9.1

Planet/ Asc	Sign	Longitude Deg:Min	Constellation	Constellation lord
Asc	Cancer	25:09	*Ashlesha*	Me
Su	Gemini	16:48	*Ardra*	Ra
Mo	Virgo	16:02	*Hasta*	Mo
Ma	Pisces	06:54	*Utrabhadrapad*	Sa
Me	Gemini	17:59	*Ardra*	Ra
Ju	Taurus	15:18	*Rohini*	Mo
Ve	Cancer	06:28	*Pushya*	Sa
Sa	Taurus	01:29	*Kritika*	Su
Ra	Virgo	02:52	*Utraphalguni*	Su
Ke	Pisces	02:52	*Poorva-bhadrapad*	Ju

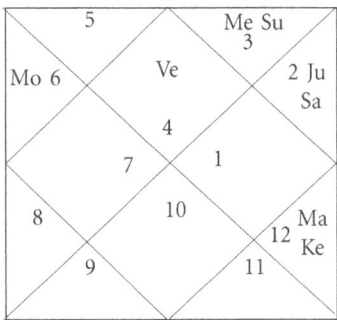

Chart 9.1: Birth chart

Dreshkaan chart for the Birth chart 9.1: The ascendant of this birth chart is Pisces 29:05. Now looking in table 10.1 under sign 12 (Pisces) in the Third row (because 29:05 falls in 20 to 30 degrees), we get sign 12, viz., Pisces so this is the ascendant sign of the dreshkaan (D/3) chart. Now in the same manner look in Table 9.1 for each of the birth chart planet and its degrees and relocate the planets. So we get the following chart as the D/3 chart for the Birth chart 9.1

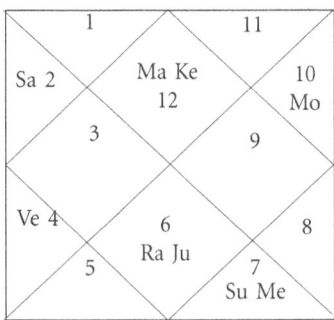

Chart 9.2: D/3 (Dreshkaan chart) for birth chart 9.1

Now keeping in mind the degrees of each planet, we can split the above D/3 chart into three charts but remember the ascendant sign will be same as we are simply splitting the above D/3 chart into three charts as per the three dreshkaans.

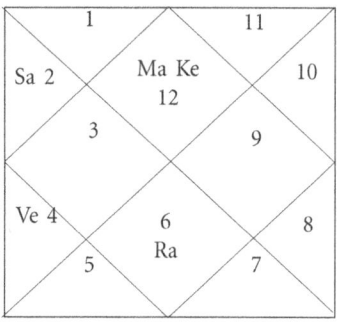

1st Dreshkaan 0–10°

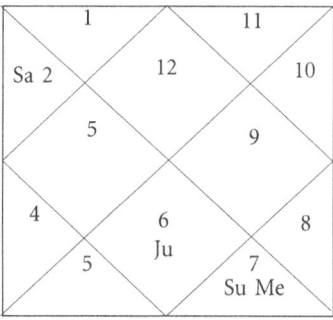

2nd Dreshkaan 10°–20°

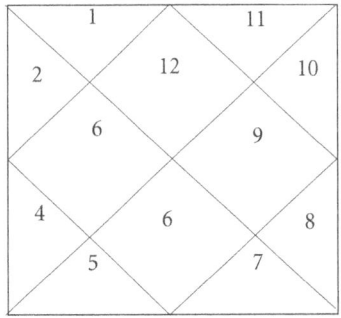

3rd Dreshkaan 20º–30º

From the Second dreshkaan chart, placement of debilitated Sun and malefic Mercury in the Eighth house confirms heart disease from which this native had suffered. Although these malefic planets here fall in the Eighth house of the Second dreshkaan chart, which represents left side of stomach, yet we need to take into consideration that the Sun which is the significator of heart is debilitated and also the longitude of both Mercury and Sun cause them to affect the next house that signifies left of chest which houses the heart.

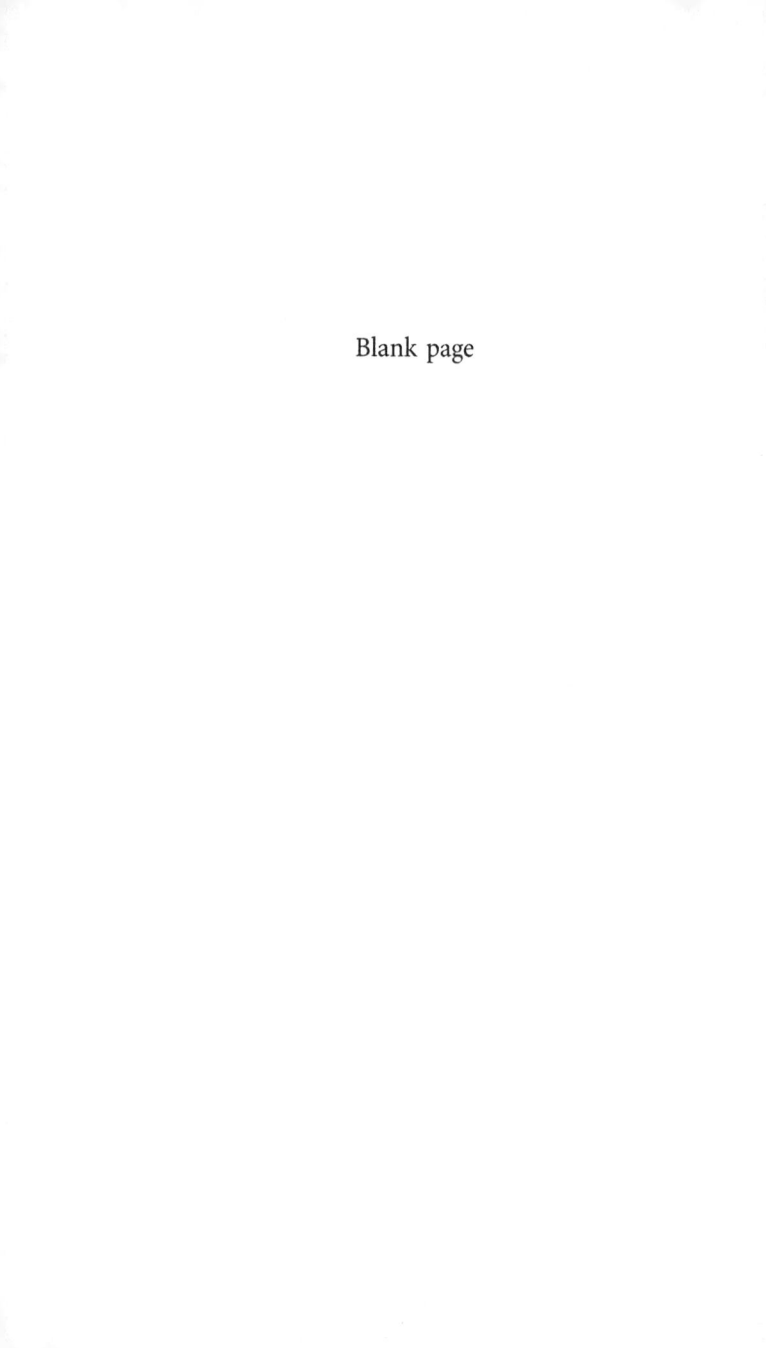

Blank page

SECTION B
Diseases

1

HEAD DISEASES

In this chapter we describe the diseases of the head. As we have already mentioned in the previous section the head houses the brain which is not only the CPU of the complex human computer, but also a relay station between the physical body and the higher self or the soul. Therefore, any damage to this part can also result in mental ailments in addition to physical ones.

One becomes prone to head diseases if, in general, the following indications are observed in a birth chart:

1. Conjunction of Rahu, Saturn and Mars in a sign.
2. Afflicted Mars placed in the ascendant.
3. Jupiter and Moon are afflicted and the ascendant lord is natural malefic.
4. Saturn as ascendant lord is placed in the ascendant and is either conjunct a malefic or aspected by one.

We will describe the following ailments of the head:

Alzheimer's disease
Brain tumour
Headaches
Meningitis
Mental problems

Alzheimer's disease: It is a progressive degenerative brain disease resulting in memory loss, loss of decision-making ability, judgement and attention. The spread of this disease can be either slow or very fast depending upon person to person. The alternative name for this disease is Senile Dementia Alzheimer's Type (SDAT). The aged people are at higher risk of getting this disease.

Symptoms include habit of repeating statements, misplacing things, getting lost even on familiar routes, personality changes, losing interest in things, hallucinations, depression, agitation, delusion, etc.

Astrological combinations are as follows:

1. The native born in the *Ashvini* constellation may become prone to this disease if a malefic planet like Mars or Rahu, Ketu falls in this constellation.
2. In a chart if Moon and Mercury are posited in the square houses and these fall in the *navamsha* of malefic planets then this disease can be predicted.

Brain tumour: In every part of human body, the cells keep dying due to wear and tear and normal new cells constantly replace these. Due to certain conditions the new cells are sometimes abnormal cells. A group of such abnormal cells in the brain is termed as a brain tumour. A brain tumour could be just a tumour and may not spread like cancer or it could in some circumstances be cancerous.

Exposure to some types of radiations, head injury or hormonal replacement therapy is some of the known causes, which could produce brain tumour. Some common symptoms are headaches, vomiting, behaviour changes, emotional instability, seizures, reduced alertness, speech difficulties, weakness, ill-feeling, obesity, and hand tremor and facial paralysis.

Astrological indications are afflictions of the ascendant and the Moon and afflictions of Mercury due to Mars. In case of brain tumours, the planet Mars also denotes need for surgery.

The following conditions also indicate tumours:

1. Afflicted Mars posited in the Scorpio sign.
2. Mars placed in the Seventh house and Saturn in the Eighth house causes tumours.
3. Saturn conjunct a malefic planet in the ascendant or aspected by a malefic gives tumours.

Headaches: Astrological indications in a chart for a headache in general are:

1. Ascendant and the ascendant lord aspected by Mars, Saturn or Rahu.
2. Sun and Mercury aspected by Saturn.

3. Malefic aspects of Mars, Saturn or Rahu or all three on the ascendant and the ascendant lord.
4. Afflictions of the Sun and Mercury due to Saturn.
5. Conjunction of Rahu, Mars and Saturn.

There is a special kind of headache called Migraine.

Migraine can be mild or very severe and is more common in women. Due to its attack one feels throbbing or pulsating sensation in the head and especially on one side of the head. In general, such an attack may last from six to forty-eight hours.

Common symptoms of migraine are:

Nausea and vomiting

Loss of appetite

Fatigue

Weakness

Increased sensitivity to light and sound

Even after the attack is over, one may feel mentally dull and sleepy with pain in the neck.

Astrological indications in a chart for migraine are:

1. Conjunction of Mars and Moon.
2. Mars placed in the ascendant under malefic influences.
3. Malefic Rahu placed in the ascendant.
4. Saturn placed in the ascendant as the ascendant lord and either conjunct or aspected by malefic planets.

Meningitis: It is an infection, which causes inflammation of the membrane covering the brain and spinal cord. Most common cause is viral infections that are cured without treatment also fungi, chemical irritation, drug allergies and tumours can lead to meningitis.

The symptoms, which indicate meningitis, are fever and chills, severe headache, nausea and vomiting, stiff neck, over sensitivity to light, rapid breathing and agitation etc.

The astrological combinations or conditions in a chart indicating meningitis are:

1. Conjunction of the ascendant and Sixth lord in the Fifth house and receiving malefic aspect of Mars.
2. Afflicted Mercury in the Sixth house aspected by Rahu and Mars.
3. The ascendant under aspect of Rahu-afflicted Mars.
4. Afflictions of Moon, Fifth and Sixth house due to Rahu and Mars.

Mental Problems

Under this heading we shall discuss the following ailments, such as Hysteria, Depression, Anger, Madness.

Hysteria: This disorder can be due to suppressed desires. The patient may become excited and start crying or shouting or become unconscious. Astrologically in a chart, the Moon and Rahu in the trik sthana-s, viz., houses Sixth, Eighth and Twelfth under malefic influences and affliction of the Fourth house indicate hysteria.

In general association of the Moon with Rahu or Ketu can lead to hysteria.

Depression: Persistent feelings of sadness, discouragement, loss of self-worth, reduced energy and concentration, sleep disorders, decreased appetite and weight loss or gain all these indicate depression.

One can suffer from depression due to many factors such as loss of spouse or a close friend or relative, sleeping difficulties, problems related to ageing, difficulty with mobility, difficulty in adapting to changed circumstances, retirement from service or some kind of brain disorder.

Some common symptoms of depression are irritable mood, sadness, feeling of worthlessness, loss of interest in life, changes in appetite, weight loss or gain, difficulty in falling asleep, fatigue, memory loss and suicidal tendency.

Depression can be diagnosed astrologically as per the following indications:

1. The Fourth house occupied by or aspected by malefics and the Fourth lord either placed in or influenced by the trik bhava-s, viz., the Sixth, Eighth and Twelfth houses.
2. The ascendant or its lord or both under affliction or a debilitated planet posited in the ascendant.
3. The Fifth house and Mercury represent the intellect. Afflictions of the Fifth house and Mercury due to Saturn give depression and feelings of despair.

Anger: Due to many conditions in life, one feels angry at times. If anger is under one's full control, then it may not be considered a disease. Some expression of anger under one's full control may be necessary to deal with certain people and situations. But it can be termed a disease if and when it becomes uncontrolled and is triggered due to very small avoidable reasons.

The following combinations in a chart indicate such problems:

1. In the chart of a native born during the daytime, if strong Mars is placed in the ascendant or the Tenth house the native becomes very angry.
2. Weak Mars placed in the ascendant or the Seventh house and receiving aspect of Saturn makes one angry.
3. The ascendant placed in the Eighth or Twelfth house gives angry nature.

Madness: A life full of tensions, fears, mental unrest and anxiety can lead to madness. Due to madness, one loses control over the senses and emotions and is unable to differentiate between good and bad.

The following astrological combinations indicate madness:

1. Conjunction of debilitated or ill-posited Saturn with Rahu or Ketu and under aspect of Mars can give madness.
2. Mercury conjunct Rahu or Saturn in the Sixth, Eighth or twelfth house and weak Moon either conjunct or aspected by Saturn.
3. Weak Moon posited in the ascendant and afflictions of the ascendant and its lord can make one mad.

4. Jupiter placed in the ascendant and Saturn in the Seventh house.
5. Weak Moon and Mercury conjunct in the ascendant.
6. Jupiter placed in the ascendant and Mars in the Seventh house.

2

EYE DISEASES

Eyes are precious and very delicate part of our body. Apart from providing vision to us, the role of eyes goes far beyond. Eyes are the doorway to our heart, and never lie. Look into the eyes of a person and you can know the state of that person's heart. The eyes easily reveal emotions such as hatred, love, jealousy, contentment, sorrow, happiness and anger.

Eyes add beauty to our personality and in case of a female, the eyes are a source of inspiration and attraction to the poetical expressions of love. The beauty of beloved's eyes has inspired poets from time immemorial.

The significators

For proper analysis of eye-related troubles from a birth chart, we need to know the houses, signs and planets, which signify eyes.

The houses: As per the kaalpurush chart, the Second and Twelfth houses represent the right and the left eye respectively.

The signs: Again referring to the kaalpurush chart, the Taurus and Pisces signs falling in the Second and Twelfth houses will represent eyes.

The planets: The main significator planets are the luminaries, viz., the Sun and the Moon. The Sun signifies the right whereas the Moon the left eye.

We may also include the lords of Taurus and Pisces signs, viz., Venus and Jupiter. Venus also signifies the eyesight or vision in general. We describe below the astrological indications about various eye related problems.

In general conjunction of the Second lord with Saturn, Mars and the sub-planet *(upgreha) mandi* gives eye diseases. Malefic planets placed in the Second and Twelfth house make the native eye-disease prone.

If the Second lord is conjunct Saturn, Mars and the sub planet *(upgreha) gulik,* eye disease can be predicted.

If the Second lord is placed in Sixth, Eighth or Twelfth place from Venus, then the native is likely to suffer from eye diseases.

Chronic eye ailments can be predicted if the Second house is heavily afflicted and receives aspect of Saturn.

Weak eyesight: The following indicate weak eyesight.

1. Sun placed in the ascendant or the Eighth house.

2. If in a chart the ascendant lord is conjunct malefics and the Second lord is under benefic aspect, then only weak eyesight can be expected.

Eye damage due to accidents:

1. Moon or Sun placed unfavourably in the Twelfth house endangers the left and the right eye respectively through accidents.
2. Saturn or Mars placed unfavourably in the Twelfth house endanger the right and the left eye respectively.
3. There is danger to the both eyes, if in a chart, Moon is conjunct three malefic planets in a sign of Venus and is not receiving any benefic aspect.
4. The ascendant lord and the Second lord occupying Sixth, Eighth or Twelfth house.
5. The left eye is endangered if weak Moon occupies the Twelfth house and does not receive any benefic aspect.
6. The right eye is endangered if the Sun is in the Twelfth house and does not receive any benefic aspect.
7. If the Moon and Venus both occupy the Twelfth house.

Blindness: The following combinations in a chart indicate chances of blindness.

1. Conjunction of the Sun and the Moon in the Twelfth house.
2. The Sixth and Eighth houses occupied by malefic planets.

3. If in a chart, Mars is in the Second house, the Moon in the Sixth house, the Sun in the Eighth and Saturn in the Ninth house.
4. Mars occupying a malefic sign.
5. The Sun placed in the Seventh house in a sign of Saturn.
6. Saturn occupying the Leo ascendant.
7. The Second and Twelfth lords and Venus and the ascendant lord all placed in trik bhavas.
8. Mars occupying the ascendant of Aquarius sign.
9. Conjunction of Saturn, Mars and Moon in a trik bhava.
10. Conjunction of the Sun and the Moon in Leo ascendant and aspected by Mars and Saturn.
11. Saturn placed in the Twelfth house, the Moon in the Second house and Sun in the Eighth house.

Cataract: It is observed that the lord of Second house posited in its own house or sign of exaltation or under other favourable conditions does not give cataract.

The following combinations indicate cataract.

1. Association of the Sun with Ketu in the Second, Twelfth, Sixth or Eighth house without receiving any benefic aspects gives inflammation of eyes resulting in cataract.
2. Sun placed in the ascendant of a watery sign gives cataract.
3. Mars placed in the ascendant and the Second house occupied by Ketu gives cataract.

EAR, NOSE AND THROAT (ENT) DISEASES

We have described in the Section-A that the nose and mouth comes under the Second house and throat and ears under the Third house. It is further believed that the right ear is represented by the Third whereas the left ear by the Eleventh house of the chart.

Diseases of Ears

Deafness:

1. If Mercury as the Third or Sixth lord is combust, then it can cause deafness.
2. The Sixth lord having any link with the planets Saturn and Mercury can cause deafness.

3. Moon and Venus conjunct and aspected by malefic planets cause deafness.
4. Conjunction of Venus and Mercury in the Twelfth house is conducive to deafness.
5. The afflictions of Jupiter and Third or Eleventh house can give problems related to right or left ears leading to deafness.

Ear problems other than deafness:

1. Conjunction of the Moon, Mars and Mercury in the Third or Eleventh house and under aspect of Ketu gives troubles in the right or left ears.
2. In the charts of Gemini and Virgo ascendants, if the Sun and Mars are conjunct in the Third, Sixth, Ninth, Eleventh or Twelfth house and don't receive any benefic aspect of Jupiter, then the native can have ear related problems.
3. The Second lord conjunct Mars in the ascendant.
4. Affliction of the Third house due to being occupied by malefic planets.
5. The Third house occupied by Mars and the sub-planet *(upgreha) gulik.*

Diseases of Nose

The diseases of the nose can be excessive sneezing, burning sensation, blocked nose or bleeding.

The significators are the Second house for the right nostril and Twelfth house for the left nostril and the airy signs, viz., Gemini, Libra and Aquarius.

Among the planets Mercury and Rahu are the main but if problem is related to the nasal bone and if there is any boil or eruption, etc., then Mars also needs to be considered.

The following astrological indications have been observed to cause nasal problems:

1. In general afflictions of Mercury can cause nasal problems.
2. The Second house or its lord under influence of the conjunction of the Sun, Mars and Saturn.
3. Moon posited in Sixth, Eighth or Twelfth house and the ascendant and Second house under affliction could lead to nasal problems.
4. Conjunction of the Moon and Mars in the ascendant can cause nose bleeding.
5. Conjunction of Mars, Venus and Saturn cause nasal problems.

Diseases of throat

Common diseases of throat are tonsils, diphtheria and dumbness.

Tonsils: Mostly it occurs in children. Sometimes fever accompanies inflammation of tonsils and there may be difficulty in swallowing food.

The planet Venus is the significator of all throat diseases.

Following astrological indications may be found in charts:

1. Afflictions of the Gemini sign due to occupation by or aspect by malefic planets.
2. The planet Mercury or the third lord under influence of malefic planets.
3. The planet Mars either posited in the third house or linked with the third lord.
4. The planet Mercury placed in the trik bhava, viz., Sixth, Eighth or Twelfth house.
5. The karaka Venus if posited in its sign of debilitation in the Twelfth house.

Diphtheria

1. The sign Gemini under malefic influence of Mars, Saturn or Rahu can give diphtheria.
2. The Third house or third lord under affliction by Mars, Saturn or Rahu.
3. The Third house under affliction and Venus, Mars and Rahu either conjunct or casting aspect on each other.

Dumbness

1. Dumbness can be caused due to afflictions of the Second house.

2. If in a charts the ascendant or its lord falls between fourteen to eighteen degrees of the signs Gemini or Sagittarius and also the planet Mercury is under the influence of Rahu-afflicted Moon, then the native may become deaf.
3. Mercury is the karaka for speech; hence its affliction can lead to dumbness.

4

NERVOUS SYSTEM DISEASES

Mercury is the significator for nerves. Therefore, its affliction or unfavourable placement in a chart can lead to nervous system-related troubles. We can also include the Moon, which is the significator of the mind.

Rahu signifies nervous disorders. Hence afflictions caused by Rahu can be the source of all nervous disorders. Rahu placed in the Cancer sign gives mental unrest and anxiety leading to nerve strain and other complications.

We describe below the combinations for some prominent nervous disorders such as paralysis, insomnia and epilepsy.

Paralysis

This is a nervous problem and is also known as *pakshaghaat, adhrang or lakva.* Due to this, either a certain portion or one side of body loses sensation and movement. The following astrological combinations indicate paralysis:

1. Debilitated Mercury placed in the ascendant and receiving aspect of Saturn.
2. Debilitated Jupiter placed in the Sixth house and receiving aspect of Saturn.
3. Combust Moon can give paralysis.
4. The Sixth house occupied by malefics, the Sixth lord under affliction and not receiving aspect of Jupiter.
5. Weak Sun conjunct Saturn, Rahu or Ketu in a trik bhava, viz., Sixth, Eighth or Twelfth house.
6. Debilitated Sixth lord conjunct Saturn in the ascendant.
7. Saturn posited in the Cancer sign and receiving aspect of Mars.
8. Sun and Venus placed in the ascendant and Saturn in the Seventh house.

Insomnia

The following symptoms indicate insomnia:

Difficulty in falling asleep, early morning awakening, interrupted sleep feeling drowsiness during the day, loud snoring, daytime fatigue, depressed feeling, anxiety, difficulty in concentrating, feeling irritable, loss of memory, etc.

The astrological indications in a chart are:

1. Debilitated Saturn posited in the ascendant and receiving aspect of the Sun.

2. The ascendant and its lord or the Sun and Moon aspected by debilitated Saturn or Mars from the Seventh house.
3. Mars or Saturn either conjunct or aspecting Sun and Moon placed in the ascendant.
4. Rahu afflicting the planet Mercury can give sleep disorders.

Epilepsy

It is a nervous disorder and is also known as seizure disorder. This is also known as *mirgi*. Due to this disease the patient has repeated fits, also called seizures. A seizure is a result of disturbed brain function. The seizure could be temporary as triggered by drugs or abnormal levels of sodium or glucose in the blood.

On the other hand, repeated seizures can be due to neurological problems and often run in a family. Some other common causes include genetic conditions at birth or injuries during or around birth, etc., diabetic complications, electrolyte imbalance, kidney failure resulting in accumulation of toxic wastes and nutritional deficiencies.

Brain infections such as meningitis and encephalitis, can also cause seizures. Epilepsy can occur at any age. Symptoms such as a tingling sensation or emotional changes occur in some people prior to a seizure. There is often confusion and weakness following a seizure.

The following astrological combinations or conditions in a chart indicate epilepsy:

1. The Moon in the Sixth house and Rahu placed in the ascendant.
2. In the chart of a native born during an eclipse, Saturn and Moon placed in the Fifth or Eighth house. But the condition is that Jupiter must not occupy a square or a trine house.
3. Conjunction of the Moon and Rahu in the Eighth house.
4. Mars aspecting the conjunction of the Moon and Saturn.

5

CHEST DISEASES

In this chapter we will describe the following diseases.

Heart diseases
Tuberculosis
Cough and cold
Asthma
Pleurisy

Heart diseases

Martin Luther described the human heart beautifully realise, 'The human heart is like a ship on a stormy sea, driven about by winds blowing from all four corners of heaven.' You will appreciate the hard work done by our heart when you realise that in a day an average heart pushes about six tons of blood through our body. The arteries supply purified blood from the heart to various parts of the body, whereas the impure blood is brought back through veins for purification by the lungs and resupplied through the heart.

On the emotional level we can say that the heart is the centre of feelings. The whole mansion of Hindi or Urdu romantic poetry will just collapse if we take away the word *dil* (heart).

Broadly speaking the following conditions indicate heart-related diseases:

1. Irregular heartbeat.
2. Blocking of the arteries.
3. Tension or pain in the muscles around the heart area.

Significators of heart diseases

For proper astrological analysis, we need to know the houses, signs and planets, which signify heart-related problems.

The houses (bhavas): As per the kaalpurush kundali (chart of time personified), the Fourth house signifies the heart.

Some believe that the Sun acts like an authority and plays an important role in general. The heart being a prominent and authoritative body part must be represented by the Sun, and as in the kaalpurush kundali the Fifth house represents the house of the Sun, therefore, the Fifth house also signifies the heart.

The signs: As per the above reasoning, it is quite clear that the signs of Cancer and Leo both signify the heart.

The planets: The Sun as we have already described and Moon because of the lordship of the Cancer sign will signify the heart. Blood is the main constituent, which is manipulated by the heart so we have to consider Mars, which signifies red corpuscles in the blood. Thus the Sun, Moon and Mars signify the heart.

The heart diseases

From the above discussion of the significators, we can conclude that afflictions and poor strength of the Sun, Moon and Mars, the Fourth and Fifth houses and their lords and the Cancer and Leo signs may lead to heart-related ailments.

Astrological conditions or combinations indicating heart diseases

1. Malefic planets placed in the Fourth house and the Fourth lord under affliction.
2. Jupiter under malefic influence of the Sun and Mars and posited in the Fourth house.
3. Weak or afflicted Moon placed in a malefic house.
4. Conjunction of the Sun and Saturn in any of the trik bhava-s, viz., Sixth, Eighth or Twelfth house.
5. Saturn placed in a square house and Moon conjunct Rahu in the Seventh house.
6. The Sun and Moon both in each other's sign or *navamsha*.

7. Conjunction of Sun and Moon in the Cancer or Leo signs.
8. Saturn placed in the Seventh house and Moon under affliction.
9. Afflicted Sun placed in the Scorpio sign.
10. Afflicted Sun falling in signs, constellations or navamshas of Saturn.
11. Sun under aspect of Saturn.
12. Sun conjunct Mars or aspected by it.
13. The Fifth lord placed in the Eighth house.
14. The Fifth house occupied by malefic planets.
15. The Sun falling in the constellations of Ketu.
16. Saturn and Sun exchanging their signs.
17. Afflictions of the watery signs, viz., Cancer, Scorpio and Pisces.
18. Conjunction of Mars and Venus in Leo sign.
19. Conjunction of Mars and Ketu in the Fourth house.
20. Conjunction of Saturn and Sun in the Fourth house.

Example 5.1: The birth chart of a native who suffered from heart disease.

Date of Birth: 2 July 1941
Place of birth: 77 E 13, 28 N 40
Time of birth: 8:30 am IST
Dasha balance at birth (Moon): Five years, Five months, and Nineteen days

Table 5.1: Planetary data for the Birth chart 5.1

Planet/ Asc	Sign	Longitude Deg:Min	Constellation	Constellation lord
Asc	Pisces	25:09	Ashlesha	Me
Su	Gemini	16:48	Ardra	Ra
Mo	Virgo	16:02	Hasta	Mo
Ma	Pisces	06:54	Utrabhadrapad	Sa
Me	Gemini	17:59	Ardra	Ra
Ju	Taurus	15:18	Rohini	Mo
Ve	Cancer	06:28	Pushya	Sa
Sa	Taurus	01:29	Kritika	Su
Ra	Virgo	02:52	Utraphalguni	Su
Ke	Pisces	02:52	Poorvabhadrapad	Ju

Table 5.2: Longitude of house cusps and constellations

House	Cusp Sign Longitude	Constellation	Constellation Lord
Fourth	Libra 21:24	Vishakha	Ju
Fifth	Scorpio 22:39	Jyeshtha	Me
Sixth	Sagittarius 23:54	Poorvaashadha	Ve

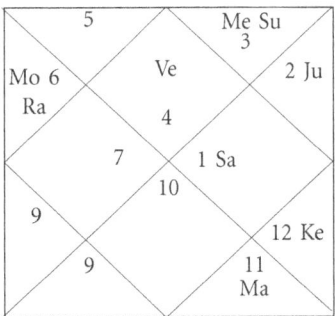

Chart 5.1: Birth chart

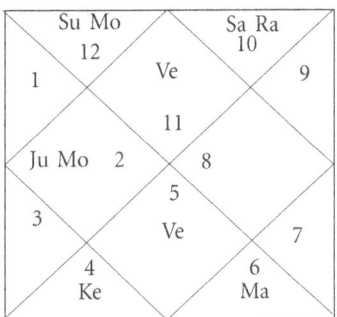

Chart 5.2: Navamsha chart

Analysis of Heart disease

For this birth chart Mercury and Venus are the malefic planets. Venus becomes more malefic for all matters concerning health because in this chart it is the lord of the obstruction house *(badhaka sthana),* viz., the Eleventh house.

Venus falls in the constellation of Saturn, which is a malefic for this chart. The Sixth house cusp also falls in the constellation of Venus. Therefore, placement of Venus in the ascendant in its enemy's house is not good for the native's health. Venus is also the Fourth lord and receives malefic aspect of Ketu. The Fifth house cusp falls in the constellation of Mercury, which is placed in the trik bhava, viz., the Twelfth house and receives aspect of Saturn.

Mars the significator of heart is posited in a trik bhava, viz., the Eighth house in birth as well as the navamsha charts and falls in the sign and constellation of malefic Saturn. Saturn is debilitated in the birth chart and falls in the inimical constellation of Sun. The significator Sun is placed in the Twelfth house and it falls in the constellation of Rahu. The Third significator planet Moon is posited in an inimical sign and is conjunct Rahu in the birth chart.

The native of this chart developed heart disease during the main period of Rahu and sub-period of Mars during the year 1971.

Tuberculosis

Tuberculosis or in short TB is also known as *raj rog, rajyakshma, yakshma* and *khshaye rog.* This disease is commonly considered a lung disease but in fact it can attack skin, marrow and blood also. Nowadays TB can be cured fully within six months time provided it is diagnosed early. The following astrological combinations indicate TB.

1. The planet Mercury placed in Cancer sign and either conjunct or aspected by a malefic can give TB.
2. The ascendant under malefic aspect of Saturn and Mars particularly when the ascendant is of a watery sign.
3. Mars aspecting the conjunction of the Moon and Saturn.
4. Conjunction of the Sun and Moon in Cancer or Leo sign and falling under malefic aspects.

Cough and Cold: Cough is quite widespread in all age groups. Accumulation of phlegm in the chest or inflammation of respiratory tract is main reasons for cough.

Various astrological indications are as follows:

1. Conjunction of Saturn and upgreha (sub-planet) gulik in the Sixth house under aspect of the Sun, Mars and Rahu.
2. Saturn aspecting the Sun placed in the Cancer sign.
3. Saturn linked with the ascendant and the Moon.
4. Conjunction of six planets, viz., the Sun, Moon, Mars, Jupiter, Venus and Saturn in a sign.
5. Conjunction of Moon and a malefic planet in the ascendant under malefic aspects.

Asthma: Asthma is a respiratory problem. The patient feels difficulty in breathing and in extreme cases under an asthmatic attack, one can feel suffocation and die if unattended.

The airy signs, viz., Gemini, Libra and Aquarius are considered related to the respiratory system. Therefore, afflictions of one or more of these signs can cause respiratory problems, like asthma.

As per the kaalpurusha chart, the lungs and respiratory tract fall under the Third house whose lord here is Mercury. Hence Mercury is the general significator of all respiratory ailments. Weak debilitated or afflicted Mercury or placed in the Sixth, Eighth or Twelfth house can give asthma.

In addition to Mercury, the Moon is the significator of phlegm and Rahu for infections.

The following combinations indicate asthma:

1. Mars aspecting the Sun placed in the ascendant.
2. The ascendant coming under aspect from Mars and Saturn.
3. Conjunction of Moon or Mercury with Rahu or Ketu in the Sixth house.
4. Venus placed in the Twelfth house and either conjunct or aspected by a malefic.
5. Moon falling in a malefic sandwich *(paapkartari)* and receiving aspect from Saturn.

Pleurisy: This is caused due to the inflammation of the covering of the lungs. Astrologically weak or afflicted Jupiter can give pleurisy.

Also in the ascendants of watery signs, viz., Cancer, Scorpio and Pisces if there is conjunction of Mars and Rahu under aspect from Saturn then the native can get this disease.

The following combinations can also give pleurisy:

1. Rahu forming any relation with the Fourth house, Fourth lord, cancer sign or Moon can give pleurisy.
2. Mars conjunct Rahu in the ascendant of a watery sign, viz., Cancer, Scorpio or Pisces and receiving aspect of Saturn can give this disease.

6

ABDOMEN DISEASES

The abdomen is also called belly and includes stomach, bowels and the digestive organs. We have included diseases related to spleen, kidneys and naval in this chapter.

Diseases of stomach

The main planet signifying stomach diseases is the Moon. The following combinations lead to stomach diseases:

1. Moon placed in the Sixth house.
2. Moon placed in the Leo sign.
3. Moon posited in the ascendant.
4. Moon placed in the ascendant and Saturn in the Eighth house.
5. The Sixth lord conjunct a malefic in the Seventh house and malefics placed in the Sixth and Eighth houses.

The stomach diseases are also known as *udar rog* and these include the following:

Lack of appetite, indigestion and weak digestive power
Diarrhoea
Irregularity of bowels and stomach cramps
Windy troubles
Dropsy
Ulcers
Worms
Stomachache

We will describe these as follows.

Lack of appetite, indigestion and low digestive power

1. Jupiter posited in the Sixth house gives lack of appetite.
2. Jupiter placed in the Third house gives low appetite.
3. Weak Sixth lord and Mars placed in the ascendant is conducive to indigestion.
4. Saturn in the Eighth house and Rahu in the First house give weak power of indigestion.
5. Affliction of the ascendant and Eighth house occupied by Saturn gives low digestive power.

Diarrhoea: This is also called *peychis or atisaar.* The following combinations in a chart indicate this disease:

1. Affliction of the Sixth lord and Venus posited in the Sixth house.
2. Conjunction of the ascendant, Fourth lord and Eighth lord.

3. Conjunction of the ascendant lord, Fourth lord and Jupiter.
4. Jupiter conjunct the ascendant lord and Eighth lord.
5. Conjunction of Mercury and Rahu in the ascendant and conjunction of Mars and Saturn in the Seventh house.
6. Conjunction of Mars, Saturn and Rahu in any house of the chart.

Irregularity of bowels and stomach cramps

1. Saturn placed in the Second house gives bowels troubles and cramps.
2. The Second house occupied by Rahu gives irregularity of bowels.

Windy troubles

1. Saturn placed in the Seventh house.
2. The Moon placed in the ascendant and Rahu or Ketu in the Seventh house.
3. The Sun placed in the ascendant and aspected by Mars.
4. Weak Fifth lord placed in the Sixth house and a weak malefic planet in the Fifth house.

Dropsy: This is also called *Jalodar.*

1. Saturn placed in the Cancer sign and the Moon in the Capricorn.

2. Rahu placed in the ascendant and conjunction of the Sun and Moon in the Tenth house.

Ulcers

Also called stomach or peptic ulcer. It is caused due to a break in the protective lining of the stomach. Common symptoms are abdominal pain, nausea, indigestion, vomitting, and blood in stool, weight loss and fatigue. Proper chewing or mastication of food items in the mouth before swallowing is very important for keeping good digestion and preventing ulcers.

If one is feeling agitated or angry, the digestive juices in the stomach become more concentrated. Therefore one should avoid eating at that time because any sharp piece of food can easily damage the protective lining inside the stomach, which then can be attacked by the concentrated digestive juices resulting in ulcers.

Astrological combinations, which indicate ulcers, are as follows:

1. Rahu placed in the Fifth house.
2. Mars placed in its sign of debilitation or in inimical sign in the Fifth house can give ulcers in the stomach or small intestines.
3. Ketu placed in the Fifth house can cause ulcers mainly due to mental worry.
4. The planet Pluto in the Fifth house can cause ulcers due to sudden upsets in life.

5. Moon either debilitated or conjunct Rahu or Ketu and associated with the Fifth house can cause ulcers.

Worms

1. Weak Moon placed in the Eighth house indicates worms in the stomach.
2. Sun placed in inimical sign can give worms during its periods.

Stomachache

1. The Eleventh lord placed in the Third house.
2. Venus posited in the Leo sign in a square or trine house and Jupiter in the Third house.
3. Moon conjunct a malefic or aspected by a malefic in the Leo sign.

Kidney-related ailments

The significators for all kidney-related ailments are the Seventh house and Libra sign and the planets Jupiter and Moon.

1. Afflicted Jupiter and Moon influencing the Seventh house, Libra sign or the Seventh lord gives kidney diseases.
2. If there is conjunction of Mars and Mercury and these are under malefic aspects and have link with Libra sign,

Seventh house or the Seventh lord then one may suffer from kidney troubles.

Naval troubles

At the naval there is a bunch of nerves and these can become misplaced leading to pain and lack of strength and mobility. The following combinations indicate this problem. One should avoid lifting heavy weights.

1. The Sixth lord placed in the Third house.
2. Conjunction of the Moon and ascendant lord in the Sixth house.

Diseases of the spleen

Spleen is also called *jigar or pleeha.* Main problem is the enlargement of spleen, which is indicated by the following combinations.

1. Conjunction of the Moon and Saturn in the Fifth house.
2. Sun placed in the Capricorn sign and Moon falling in between Saturn and Mars.
3. Afflictions of the Moon and the Sixth lord.
4. Saturn placed in the ascendant, Fourth or Seventh house in the chart of a native born at night during the dark phase of the Moon.

7

REPRODUCTIVE – ORGANS DISEASES

In the *Bhagavad Gita,* the sacred and valuable scripture of India, Lord Krishna tells that it is the unfulfilled desires, which keep us earth bound for many incarnations.

Human beings are ever engrossed in the deep sea of endless desires. Our wise sages categorised all desires under three distinct headings as follows.

Lokeshna (desire for name and fame)
Vitteshna (desire for immense material wealth)
Putreshna (desire for progeny particularly sons)

But life on earth is meant for learning and evolving and also the karmic balance from previous existence needs to be worked out. Because of these reasons, a native may have astrological combinations in the birth chart, which deprive him or her, to fulfil any of the above desires in a particular incarnation. Any defect in the reproductive organs or system can deprive one from putreshna or the desire to have progeny in order to carry forward one's family.

We describe below some prominent diseases and their indicative combinations in the birth chart.

Impotency: All causes, which prevent a man from making women pregnant, fall under impotency. These can be underdeveloped male organ, inability of the male organ to become erect, low sperm count and premature ejaculation. The following astrological combinations indicate problems related to impotency.

1. Conjunction of Venus and Saturn in the Tenth house.
2. Saturn placed in the Sixth or Twelfth house with respect to Venus.
3. In a chart of Virgo ascendant Saturn placed in the ascendant and Mercury conjunct Rahu or Ketu in the Seventh house.
4. Conjunction of Mercury Saturn and Rahu in the ascendant or the Seventh house.
5. Conjunction of Venus and Saturn in the Third, Eighth or Eleventh house.
6. Venus placed in the Eighth house under aspect of Saturn.

Infertility: Inability of a woman to become pregnant due to problems in her reproductive or fertility mechanism is termed as infertility.

The following astrological combinations are indicative of such problems.

1. Sun and Saturn conjunct in the Eighth house.
2. Mercury alone placed in the Eighth house.
3. Conjunction of the Moon, Venus and Saturn in the ascendant and Fifth house under affliction.
4. Conjunction of the Moon, Venus and Saturn in the ascendant and Fifth house under affliction.

Ailments related to menstrual cycle

1. A malefic planet placed in the ascendant and the Sixth house occupied by two malefic planets.
2. The Seventh lord under affliction.
3. The Seventh and Eighth lords linked to Sixth house or Sixth lord.

Ailments of male reproductive organ

1. The Eighth house under heavy affliction.
2. The Eighth lord receiving aspect of Rahu.
3. The ascendant lord and Mars conjunct in the Sixth house.
4. Conjunction of Sixth lord and Mars in any house.
5. Combust Mars in the Eighth house can cause diseases of genitals.

Involuntary abortion: Because of some medical problems abortion can occur on its. Following combinations indicates such probability.

1. The Fifth lord placed in a malefic house and the Fifth house under affliction.
2. Affliction of the Fifth house of the navamsha chart.
3. Association of Mars, Rahu with Fifth house can cause miscarriage and abortion.
4. If in a female chart the Fifth house falls between the planets Rahu and Mars, there are chances of abortion or miscarriage.

Leucorrhoea: This is the discharge of a white fluid from the vagina.

1. The planets Rahu or Saturn aspecting the Eighth house.
2. Venus receiving malefic aspects.
3. Venus conjunct a trik bhava lord, viz., lord of Sixth, Eighth or Twelfth house.
4. Moon placed in the Seventh house can give this disease.
5. Conjunction of Moon and Venus in the ascendant.
6. Moon placed in the Seventh house and Venus in the ascendant.
7. Conjunction of Seventh lord and a malefic planet in an inimical sign.

Enlarged Prostrate: Prostrate gland in males produces the seminal fluid that carries the sperms. This gland surrounds the tube through which urine moves. Almost in all males, as they get older, this gland enlarges and causes problems related to urination and bladder. In the medical language, enlarged prostrate is called Benign Prostate Hyperplasic (BPH) or Benign Prostate Hypertrophy. It is not cancerous.

Some of the common symptoms are weak urine system such as urine keeps dribbling after urination, strong and sudden urge to urinate and incomplete emptying of the bladder and pain with urination.

The significators for prostrate-related troubles is the Scorpio sign and planets Venus and Mars.

1. Rahu afflicting the Scorpio sign or Venus and Mars can give prostrate enlargement.
2. Mars placed in the Taurus sign can give prostrate-related troubles.

Hydrocele: A disease of the testicles in which the testicles get enlarged due to water. The following combinations indicate this disease.

1. Afflictions of the Eighth house.
2. Conjunction of Rahu with Saturn or Mars in the ascendant.
3. Conjunction of Mars and Venus in the Eighth house.
4. Affliction of the Eighth house and Venus under aspect from Rahu.

Miscellaneous sexual diseases: The following combinations indicate some sexual diseases as described below:

1. Conjunction of the ascendant lord with Rahu in the Eighth house can cause problems related to ovaries in women.

2. Association of Rahu with the planets Saturn and Mars can give venereal diseases.
3. Ketu placed in the Sixth house under unfavourable conditions can give venereal diseases.
4. In a female chart, association of Venus with Mars, Rahu, Sixth lord or Sixth house can give troubles related to the womb.

8

DISEASES OF LEGS AND FEET

Ailments or problems of the legs

One can have injury in the legs, born lame or have some other deformation in the legs. The following combinations indicate these:

1. Placement of strong Moon and Mars in the Sixth house can give injury to the legs.
2. Conjunction of Saturn, Moon and Mars in the Twelfth house can give injury in the upper part of legs.
3. Conjunction of Saturn and the Sixth lord in the Twelfth house and aspected by a malefic planet indicates lameness from birth.
4. Conjunction of the Sun, Mars and Saturn in the Sixth house may appear in the chart of a native born lame.

5. Sun and Mars placed in the Eleventh house can cause some deformity in the legs.
6. Afflicted Saturn in the Sixth, Eighth or Twelfth house causes leg injury.

Arthritis

It is inflammation of a joint resulting in pain and swelling and difficult movement of the joint. Arthritis is also known as joint inflammation. In normal conditions cartilage protects a joint against friction and shocks, if this cartilage breaks down, then there is friction in the joint bones which results in pain, swelling and stiffness. Joint inflammation can also occur due to a broken bone, infection, immune system disorder or general wear and tear.

Osteo-arthritis is more common and results because of age and common joints affected due to this are hip joint, knees and fingers. Arthritis can occur in men and women of all ages. You can suspect arthritis if there is pain or swelling in a joint, stiffness especially in the morning hours, warm feeling or redness around a joint and difficulty in moving that joint.

The following combinations indicate problems related to knee joints.

1. Conjunction of full Moon and Mars in the Sixth house can give pain in knees.
2. Conjunction of Saturn, Moon and Mars in the Twelfth house gives knee troubles.

3. Saturn as the Seventh lord conjunct a malefic planet.
4. Conjunction of the Moon and Saturn in Cancer sign and not receiving any benefic aspect.
5. The Sun placed in Cancer sign and aspected by Saturn.
6. Weak Moon and Saturn placed in the Twelfth house
7. Conjunction of the Sixth lord and Rahu or Ketu in the ascendant.

Defects or troubles in the feet

1. Conjunction of the Moon and a malefic planet in the Cancer, Scorpio or Pisces sign gives defective feet.
2. Afflictions of the Aries, Cancer, Scorpio and Pisces signs can cause defects in feet.
3. Afflicted Saturn falling in Leo navamsha can give feet injuries.
4. Rahu falling in the navamsha of Saturn gives troubles related to feet.

9

CANCER

Life and death exists side by side. Each day millions of our body cells die or get worn out and these are continually being replaced by new cells. All new cells are not healthy; also toxins keep depositing particularly more in such unhealthy cells and set out a sort of uncontrolled growth, which takes the form of cancer.

Cancer can occur in any part of the body but generally in males, cancer of lungs, mouth, larynx, colon, prostrate gland, digestive system and bone marrow is common. Females are more prone to cancer of breast, cervix, food pipe, ovaries, uterus and stomach.

Anyone of the following can cause cancer:

1. Exposure to radiations
2. Overexposure to sunlight
3. Tobacco – cigarette smoking or eating tobacco

4. Certain viruses
5. Chemical benzene
6. Eating certain poisonous mushrooms

Cancer is a sort of poison in the body and the planet Rahu signifies poison in astrology. Therefore the main karaka or significator of this disease is Rahu. It has been observed that in case of slow developing cancer weak or afflicted Jupiter can come into the picture whereas any rapid developments are more so due to Rahu.

There can be different astrological conditions involving any planet and house but the role of Rahu, trik bhava-s (the Sixth, Eighth and Twelfth houses), the Sixth lord play a crucial and decisive role in this disease.

Placement of the Sixth lord in the ascendant, Eighth or the Tenth house and its association with Rahu increases the chances of getting this disease.

Similarly, influence of Rahu over the trik bhavas, viz., Sixth, Eighth or Twelfth houses or association of malefic Rahu with any weak or afflicted planet in a particular house tends to cause cancer in the relevant part of the body.

The planet Saturn in general signifies sorrow and suffering and Mars is associated with boils and surgery. The Eighth house in a chart is for unseen and unexpected troubles and difficulties, etc. Hence if in a chart Saturn is linked in any manner with the ascendant or the Eighth house and Mars then the chances of getting cancer increases manifold.

The Table 9.1 indicates the body part that may develop cancer corresponding to all the weak and Rahu afflicted planets:

Table 9.1: Table indicating body part under threat corresponding to each afflicted planet

Planet afflicted by Rahu or weak in strength	Body part under threat of cancer
Sun	Head (brain), heart, stomach and blood
Moon	Marrow, blood, breast and heart
Mars	Blood, bone marrow, reproductive organs, uterus and neck
Mercury	Nose, mouth and umbilicus
Jupiter	Ears, liver, thigh
Venus	Throat, reproductive organs
Saturn	Hands, feet, legs, gums
Ketu	Head, neck and blood

Some combinations indicating cancer

1. In the chart of Cancer ascendant, if Jupiter as the Sixth lord is under aspect of Eighth lord Saturn and the ascendant lord Moon is associated with Saturn and Rahu or Ketu, then there are chances of getting cancer.
2. If the Third lord is placed in the Eighth and aspected by the Sixth lord and Mars and Saturn. And Rahu aspecting the ascendant gives cancer.
3. Conjunctions or associations of Jupiter, Mars and Saturn
4. Weak or afflicted the Sun particularly when posited in

the Third house or aspected by or conjunct Third lord sets a background for a serious disease like cancer.

5. Affliction of watery signs, viz., Cancer, Scorpio or Pisces can be a reason for getting cancer.

6. Affliction of the Moon can give cancer or blood-related diseases.

7. Conjunction of Venus, Jupiter and Ketu

8. Ascendant lord and Moon under affliction or weak in strength.

9. Saturn conjunct Mars and posited opposite Jupiter or Rahu.

10. Afflictions of the ascendant, the Sun and Moon.

11 Afflicted Sixth or Eighth lord placed in the ascendant.

12. Mars placed in the Sixth house in a fixed sign, viz., Taurus, Leo, Scorpio or Aquarius.

13. Afflictions of watery signs, viz., Cancer, Scorpio and Pisces and Moon causes blood cancer.

14. Placement of the Sixth lord in the Eighth or Tenth house along with malefic planets and not receiving any benefic aspect.

15. Presence of kaalsarpa yoga and the Sun being afflicted may give cancer.

16. Heavy afflictions of the Moon and Venus can give cancer in the stomach.

17. In a female chart, the Moon associated with or aspected by Saturn and Mars can give cancer of breast or uterus.

18. Conjunction of the Moon and Saturn and these falling in the navamsha of Cancer, Scorpio or Aquarius.

19. Either node, viz., Rahu or Ketu placed at the Third, Sixth, Eighth, or Twelfth place from Mars or Saturn or both creates strong chances for getting cancer.
20. In cases of throat cancer, the Moon is found to be with malefics under heavy afflictions.

The following observations are gathered from charts of cancer patients having cancer in different parts:

Kidney cancer: Malefic influences on the fixed signs particularly Taurus or Scorpio and especially the area between two to ten degrees of these signs. A weak Moon afflicted by Rahu can cause kidney cancer.

Spine cancer: For spinal cancer the malefic influence over the following has been observed:

1. Around twenty-six degrees of cancer and Capricorn signs.
2. Dual signs, viz., Gemini, Virgo, Sagittarius or Pisces.
3. First degree of Saturn.

Marrow cancer: Afflictions of the Sun, Saturn, Tenth house and Capricorn sign.

Blood cancer

1. Afflictions of the Moon and Mars cause blood cancer.
2. Association of the watery signs, viz., Cancer, Scorpio and Pisces with the Sixth house and or Rahu can cause cancer of blood.
3. Debilitated Mars aspected by Rahu or Sixth lord can cause blood cancer.

Spleen cancer: Afflictions of the Moon and Rahu.

Lung cancer: Third house, Gemini sign and first four degrees of Aries and Libra signs under affliction.

Breast cancer: It occurs in the breast tissues. There are mainly two types one is ductile carcinoma, which occurs in the ducts through which milk moves, and it is a common type. The second type occurs in lobules that produce milk and it is called lobular carcinoma.

In rare cases, breast cancer can occur in other portions of the breast. The risk of developing breast cancer increases with age. In cases of breast cancer the Fourth house, Rahu or its depositor, Saturn and Moon play important role.

Example 9.1: The birth chart of a native who suffered from Brain Cancer.

Date of Birth: 2 Mar 1961
Place of birth: 76 E 24, 30 N 19
Time of birth: 22:10 Hours IST
Dasha balance at birth (Venus): Ten years, Zero months, and Four days

Table 9.1: Planetary data for the Birth chart 9.1

Planet/ Asc	Sign	Longitude Deg:Min	Constellation	Constellation lord
Asc	Cancer	08:19	*Swati*	Ra
Su	Aquarius	18:34	*Shatbhisha*	Ra

Mo	Leo	19:59	*Poorvaphalguni*	Ve
Ma	Gemini	10:01	*Ardra*	Ra
Me (R)	Aquarius	02:03	*Dhanishtha*	Ma
Ju	Capricorn	04:17	*Utraashadha*	Su
Ve	Aries	00:01	*Ashvini*	Ke
Sa	Capricorn	03:03	*Utraashadha*	Su
Ra	Leo	12:56	*Magha*	Ke
Ke	Aquarius	12:56	*Shatbhisha*	Ra

Table 9.2: Longitude of house cusps and constellations

House	Cusp Sign Longitude	Constellation	Constellation Lord
6th	Pisces 09:12	*Utrabhadrapad*	Sa

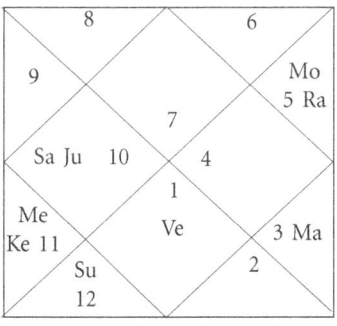

Chart 9.1: Birth chart

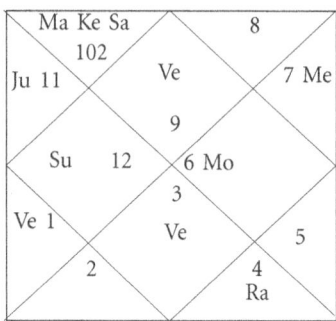

Chart 9.2: Navamsha chart

Analysis of Brain Cancer

The brain is signified by the ascendant, its lord and the planet Sun. In the birth chart the ascendant lord Venus is posited in the inimical sign of Aries, however the sign Aries represents the head or brain as per the kaalpurusha chart. Venus in the navamsha chart also is placed in Aries sign. Venus falls in the malefic constellation of Ketu. Venus is further afflicted due to aspect of Rahu confirming cancer in the head area.

The karaka Sun is also a badhaka planet or planet of obstruction for this chart. Sun is posited in inimical sign and constellation and is conjunct Ketu and aspected by Rahu.

Jupiter for this chart is a functional malefic, it is Sixth lord and debilitated. Its conjunction with Saturn indicates long suffering however Saturn is not a malefic for this chart and it is posited in own sign. Because of this, the native's disease has been cured after surgery because of propitiation of Jupiter and the Sun, as directed by the author.

10

SKIN DISEASES

The planet Mercury represents skin and it is particularly so if Mercury is associated with the ascendant. Saturn is the main significator of disease and the Moon, which represents blood, plays an important role in all skin ailments in general. Since the planet Mercury is a significator of skin, sub-periods of Mercury during the main periods of the Sun can give skin diseases.

Here we describe the following skin diseases:
Eczema
Pimples, boils and tumour
Leprosy
Leucoderma

Eczema

It is also called Atopic Dermatitis and is a chronic skin disorder and produces scaly and itching rashes. Eczema is

very common in infants. It is a sort of allergy, which causes inflammation, and the skin becomes itchy and scaly.
Common symptoms are intense itching, blisters, skin redness and rashes.

The following astrological indications show eczema:

1. Moon placed in a watery sign and aspected by Saturn placed in a watery sign.
2. If the Sun is placed in the ascendant and it is either conjunct a malefic or aspected by one then it can cause skin problems like eczema.
3. Conjunction of Mars and Saturn in the Third house.
4. If the Moon is conjunct a malefic in the Ninth house then it can cause itching.

Pimples, boils and tumour

1. Conjunction of the Sixth lord with Rahu or Ketu in the Eighth house can give boils on the lips.
2. Conjunction of Sixth lord with Saturn in the Eighth house gives boils or wounds in the feet.
3. Conjunction of the ascendant lord with Mars in the trik bhavas, viz., Sixth, Eighth or Twelfth house gives a tumour.

Leprosy

In this disease, mainly the planets Moon, Mars, Mercury, Saturn and Rahu play an important role. Venus being the significator of beauty also comes into picture. The following combinations show leprosy.

1. The Sixth lord posited in the Seventh house and either conjunct or aspected by Ketu.
2. Conjunction of Moon and Mars in the Seventh house and under aspect of Saturn or Ketu.
3. Conjunction of the ascendant lord, Sixth lord and Eighth lord in the Sixth house.
4. Association of Saturn with one or more out of the ascendant, Mars, Rahu and Moon.
5. Sun placed in the Leo sign and under aspect of Venus.
6. Conjunction or association of the ascendant lord, Mercury and Moon with Rahu or Ketu.
7. Conjunction of Sun, Venus and Saturn in any house of the chart.
8. Placement of Mars in the ascendant and Sun placed in the Eighth and Saturn in the Fourth house.
9. Placement of the Moon, Mars, Jupiter, Venus and Saturn in watery signs, viz., Cancer, Scorpio or Pisces.
10. Sun posited in the Aries or Scorpio sign and under aspect from Venus.

Leucoderma

It is a blood-generated skin disorder and is popularly known in India as *phulvehri*. The main significators are the Moon, Saturn and Mercury. Some combinations, which have been observed in the charts, are given below:

1. Conjunction of the ascendant lord, Moon and Rahu or Ketu in any house.
2. Conjunction of the Moon and Rahu.
3. Mars conjunct another malefic planet in the ascendant.
4. Conjunction of the Moon and Venus under malefic influence in a watery sign.

Example 10.1: The birth chart of a native who is suffering from leucoderma (phulvehri) disease

Date of Birth: 31 Mar 1949
Place of birth: 74 E 34, 28 N 41
Time of birth: 06:30 Hours IST
Dasha balance at birth (Ketu): Five years, Ten months, and Twelve days

Table 10.1: Planetary data for the Birth chart 10.1

Planet/ Asc	Sign	Longitude Deg:Min	Constellation	Constellation lord
Asc	Pisces	17:44	*Revati*	Me
Su	Pisces	16:51	*Revati*	Me
Mo	Aries	02:09	*Ashvini*	Ke
Ma	Pisces	13:56	*Utrabhadrapad*	Sa
Me	Pisces	03:53	*Utrabhadrapad*	Sa
Ju	Capricorn	05:15	*Utraashadha*	Su
Ve	Pisces	12:30	*Utrabhadrapad*	Sa
Sa	Leo	07:00	*Magha*	Ke
Ra	Aries	02:27	*Ashvini*	Ke
Ke	Libra	02:27	*Chitra*	Ma

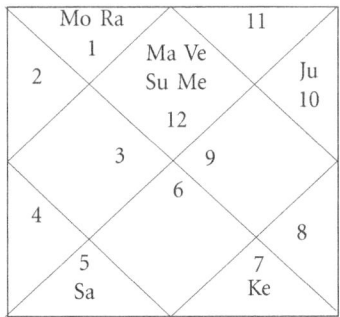

Chart 10.1: Birth chart

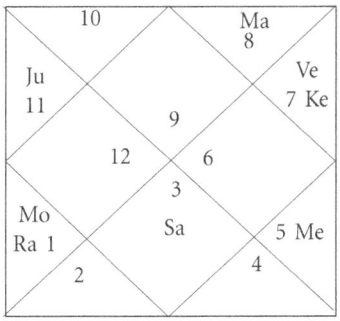

Chart 10.2: Navamsha chart

Analysis of Leucoderma

One of the karaka for this disease, viz., Moon is conjunct Rahu in the Second house, which indicates this disease affecting the face of the native.

This conjunction also exists in the same sign in the navamsha chart, which further aggravates the disease. Moon falls in the malefic constellation of Ketu.

The Sixth lord Sun is conjunct the karaka of beauty Venus and karaka of skin, viz., Mercury in the ascendant and all these are further associated due to conjunction with Mars.

In the above chart, the planet Mercury very distinctly and strongly represents skin as it is posited in the ascendant and the ascendant itself falls in the constellation of Mercury.

Venus is also afflicted in the navamsha chart

11

MISCELLANEOUS DISEASES

Some diseases, not described in the previous chapters, are discussed here.

Blood disorders

There are many diseases of the blood, such as leukaemia, which is a bone marrow disease and causes uncontrolled increase in the white blood cells, which are called leukocytes. Another common problem is anaemia. The oxygen carrying part of the red blood cells is called haemoglobin and anaemia is a condition where there is a lower than normal haemoglobin counts in the blood. Common symptoms are chest pain, shortness of breath and fatigue.

For the above ailments the astrological combinations are as follows:

1. Mars conjunct sub-planet gulik in the Second or Eighth house.

2. If Mars is debilitated, combust or placed in inimical sign then blood disease are expected.
3. Saturn placed in the ascendant and Moon placed in Sixth or Tenth house and receiving aspect from Mars.
4. The Second lord is either conjunct Mars or aspected by Mars.

Hypertension: This means high blood pressure. The blood pressure is measured in millimetres of mercury (mm Hg). The blood pressure reading is written as two figures for example 120 over 80 or written as 120/80. The numerator figure is the systolic pressure or the pressure when the heart beats. The denominator represents the diastolic pressure inside the blood vessels during the periods when the heart is at rest. The safe limits are also subject to age but the systolic pressure is considered high if it stays over 140 and diastolic is considered high if it stays over 90.

If you observe over a couple of readings the systolic blood pressure between 120 and 139 or the diastolic blood pressure between 80 and 89 then this condition is called pre-hypertension and you are likely to develop high blood pressure.

Factors, which affect blood pressure, are amount of water and salt in the body, condition of kidneys, condition of nervous system, condition of blood vessels and level of different body hormones.

Some common symptoms are mild headache, confusion, and chest pain, buzzing noise in the ear, irregular heartbeat, nosebleed, change of vision and feeling tired.

Astrological combinations, which indicate high BP, are as follows:

In blood pressure-related problems, the planets Moon and Mars play an important role.

1. Conjunction of Mars and upgreha (sub-planet) gulik in either the Second or the Eighth house.
2. If the planet Mars is combust, weak or posited in the sign of debilitation or its enemy.
3. The Second lord either conjunct or aspected by Mars.
4. Mars placed in the Second house and receiving aspect of the Sun.
5. It has been observed in some charts that even Jupiter under heavy affliction and forming link with Moon tends to give high blood pressure.
6. Affliction of the Moon by Mars.
7. The Fourth and Fifth lords having links with the trik bhavas, viz., Sixth, Eighth or Twelfth house or with Mars, Saturn, Rahu or Ketu or the Third lord tend to give high BP.
8. If the Moon is weak and the watery signs are afflicted and the planets Saturn and Mars are related to the Sixth house.
9. If the watery signs are afflicted and Saturn afflicts the Fourth house and the Fourth lord is placed in the Eighth house then high blood pressure can be expected.

Piles

This is also known as *arsh rog*.

1. Saturn placed in the Twelfth house under malefic aspects.
2. The Eighth lord and a malefic planet conjunct in the Seventh house.
3. The Sixth lord conjunct a malefic in the Eighth house.
4. Conjunction of Mars, Mercury and ascendant lord in Leo sign in the Fourth or Twelfth house of a chart.

Diabetes

As the food we eat is digested a sugar called glucose goes into the bloodstream. This sugar acts as a source of energy. Insulin produced by the pancreas helps in moving this sugar from bloodstream into muscles, fat and liver cells. But when the pancreas does not make enough insulin, the level of blood sugar rises and diabetes sets in.

One should get medical check up if any of the following symptoms appear:

Frequent urination, increased thirst, weight loss, fatigue, increased appetite, blurred vision, slow healing infections, male impotency, and nausea and vomiting.

The astrological combinations showing diabetes are as follows:

1. Jupiter falling in the sign or constellation of Saturn and receiving malefic aspects.

2. Jupiter either conjunct Saturn or receiving its aspect.
3. Afflictions of the Eighth house and one or more out of Jupiter, Venus and Moon under affliction.
4. The Eighth lord conjunct Rahu particularly in the Third or Eighth house.
5. Mercury posited in the Sagittarius or Pisces sign and receiving aspect from Sun.
6. The Sun placed in the ascendant and Mars in the Seventh house.
7. Conjunction of the Sun, Saturn and Venus in the Fifth house.

Hernia: This disease is to be diagnosed from Libra sign, Seventh house and the planet Moon.

The following combinations can cause hernia:

1. Weak and afflicted Moon having association with Seventh house or Libra sign.
2. Weak Moon falling in watery navamsha.
3. Association of the Seventh lord or Seventh house with Sixth lord or Sixth house.

Dental diseases: The dentures fall under the Taurus sign and Second house of the kaalpurusha chart. Saturn signifies the teeth and the Sun is the general significator for bones.

We can conclude that if in a chart the Second house, its lord, the Taurus sign, are under affliction or related to the house of disease or trik bhavas, viz., Sixth, Eighth and Twelfth houses then dental problems can be expected.

Afflictions caused by Rahu can give long teeth, which decay early. Afflictions by Mars can give bleeding of gums and need for surgery and Saturn can cause dental decay and disease such as pyorrhoea.

Apart from these, the following combinations also indicate dental diseases:

1. If in a chart Saturn, Sun and Moon are placed in the Seventh house and do not receive any benefic aspect then dental problems can occur.
2. Rahu or Ketu posited in the Sixth house.
3. Saturn posited in the ascendant in a sign other than its own could give dental problems.

SECTION C
Cure

REMEDIAL MEASURES

If there is a problem, there also exists its solution. Problems or obstacles are there to test our level of patience and tolerance in order to develop equanimity or balance of mind. Also, it is a fact that human beings learn better and fast if beset with problems. The gold ore may think that it is being tortured needlessly by putting it in a furnace but the beautiful ornament when made out of it can look back and smile.

Prevention is better than cure

It is always better and wise to take timely steps in order to prevent a disease or injury. This is possible only if we take the trouble of getting the birth chart analysed in detail beforehand. One can with the knowledge contained in this book pinpoint the planets, which can cause health-related problems during their main or sub-periods and unfavourable transits.

Diagnosis

The next step is to find out which of these planets are favourable or benefic for the native and which are unfavourable or malefic. The remedial measures, such as wearing gemstones or items governed by planets, help boost the strength of the relevant planet. The remedial measures such as recitation of mantras, worship, prayers, giving alms *(daan),* etc., help propitiate the relevant planet and make them favourable to the native.

Then there are some short-cut methods also called *totkaas*, which are quite effective in curing particular problems. There is another system in which gemstones are recommended based on their curative powers just to cure specific ailments; this system does not take into consideration the functional nature of the planets for the particular chart. The author suggests that one should not mix the two systems and just follow any one system with full faith.

Boosting the strength of favourable planets by gemstones

As per this system the gemstones are worn corresponding to the benefic planet, which needs to be boosted in strength. Table 1.1 shows gemstones for each of the nine planets.

Table 1.1: Gemstones for the nine planets

Planet	Gemstone (English Name)	Gemstone (Hindi Name)
Sun	Ruby	*Maanik*
Moon	Pearl	*Moti*
Mars	Red Coral	*Moonga*
Mercury	Emerald	*Panna*
Jupiter	Yellow Sapphire	*Pukhraaj*
Venus	Diamond	*Heera*
Saturn	Blue Sapphire	*Neelam*
Rahu (North node of the Moon)	Hessonite	*Gomed*
Ketu (South node of the Moon)	Cat's Eye-Chrysoberyl Or Cymophane	*Lehsunia*

The above gemstones can be set in the relevant metal as per Table 1.2.

Table 1.2: Metals assigned to planets.

Lord Planet	Metal
Sun	Gold
Moon	Silver
Mars	Copper or Gold

Table cont.

Lord Planet	Metal
Mercury	Gold
Jupiter	Gold
Venus	Platinum or gold
Saturn	Iron or lead
Rahu (North node of the Moon)	*Alloy of five metals
Ketu (South node of the Moon)	– Do –

*Alloy of silver, gold, copper, iron and zinc, also called panchdhaatu.

The ring containing the gemstone can be worn on the appropriate finger as per Table 1.3.

Table 1.3: Appropriate finger for wearing the gemstone

Lord Planet	Name of the Finger	
	Hindi	English
Sun	Anamika	Ring finger
Moon	Kanishtha	Small finger
Mars	Anamika	Ring finger
Mercury	Kanishtha	Small finger
Jupiter	Tarjani	First finger

Venus	*Anamika or Madhyama*	Ring or Middle finger
Saturn	*Madhyama*	Middle finger
Rahu (north node of the Moon)	*Madhyama*	Middle finger
Ketu (south node of the Moon)	*Kanishtha* or Madhyama	Small or middle finger

Prescribing gemstones to cure diseases

Note: *If you follow these then do not bother about the functional nature of corresponding planets in the birth chart, as this system is not based on a birth chart.*

These are general prescriptions which are based on time-tested healing and disease-curing properties of precious as well as semi-precious gemstones. Some of these general prescriptions are given below:

Heart ailments: Moonstone is good for curing mental tension, blood pressure and heart problems. Pearl cures blood pressure problems and palpitation of heart. Ruby, hessonite and turquoise are also good for heart ailments. Agate and Jade give strength to heart.

Asthma: Jade and tiger's eye are good for asthmatic ailments. For chronic ailment, wear emerald in the ring finger and white coral in the middle finger of right hand.

Diabetes: White coral, white sapphire and emerald are good for curing diabetes. For curing chronic problems, wear yellow sapphire in the first finger and white coral in the middle finger of right hand.

Stones in the kidney: Malachite also called 'kidney stone' is good for curing stones in the kidney. Indian name of 'kidney stone' is *daana phirang*.

Headache and migraine: Jade and turquoise are good for these problems.

Insomnia: Moonstone, emerald and yellow sapphire are good for curing insomnia.

Piles: Bloodstone is good for curing piles.

Respiratory problems of children: Cat's eye chrysoberyl is believed to cure respiratory problems of children, if worn as a pendant.

AIDS: Turquoise and yellow sapphire.

Hernia: Red coral and topaz *(pokhraj)*.

Curing by energising the spinal spiritual *chakras*

Along the spinal cord there are seven subtle energy centres called chakras. These are not physical but exist on the astral plane. Through these centres, energy from higher bodies, flow to the physical body.

Table 1.4: Curing with crystals by energising the relevant spiritual spinal *chakra*

Name of Chakra	Location	Ailments	Crystals to be used
The root chakra or Mooladhar chakra:	The exact location of this first centre is half-way between the organ of excretion and organ or reproduction	This centre controls kidneys, bladder, spine, body strength, awareness and vitality. If this centre is unbalanced, apart from the ailments connected with the above, one may also feel sad and lethargic.	(1) Agate of red colour (2) Bloodstone (3) Ruby (4) Smoky Quartz
The sacral chakra or Swadhishthan chakra	At the genitalia level	Ailments related to phlegm and cold, urinary troubles, bed-wetting, sexual diseases, inflammation of the body, etc.	(1) Carnelian (2) Sunstone (3) Calcite
The solar plexus chakra or Manipur chakra	At the level of the umbilicus or navel	It controls stomach, liver, and gall bladder and body temperature. This is the centre of strength and bliss. If this centre is imbalanced there may be skin diseases, blood related diseases, loose motions, indigestion, acidity, gastric problems and diabetes.	(1) Topaz (2) Amber (3) Tiger's eye (4) Citrine (5) Yellow Zircon (6) Yellow Sapphire *(Table cont.)*

Name of Chakra	Location	Ailments	Crystals to be used
The heart chakra or Anahat chakra	Located in the centre of the chest at the heart level	If this centre is unbalanced there can be problems related to the nervous system, heart and blood pressure. One may have bodily pains, depression, pessimistic outlook and tendency to commit suicide.	(1) Emerald (2) Jade (3)Malachite (4) Rose-Quartz
The throat chakra or Vishudha chakra	At the level of the throat	If this centre is unbalanced all the three bodily humours are upset. This centre controls the throat, lungs, speech and expression.	(1) Blue Sapphire (2) Celestite (3) Turquoise (4) Aquamarine
The brow chakra or Ajna chakra	At the eyebrow level between the eyes	This is the centre of will power and inspiration. Development of this centre gives clairvoyance, telepathic ability and super natural knowledge. A strong will help greatly in keeping fit.	(1)Amethyst (2) Sodalite (3) Lapis Lazuli (4) Azurite
The Crown chakra or Sahasrara chakra	The centre of the head.	This is the centre of spiritual power and is related to the Pineal gland. By developing this centre one can open up a channel through which	(1) Rock crystal (2) Flourite

Propitiating by giving alms (daan)

It is believed that by giving things belonging to a planet to a needy person one can propitiate the concerned planet. For better results give alms for a planet on the day governed by it. For example Sunday for the Sun, Monday for the Moon, Tuesday for Mars and Ketu, Wednesday for Mercury, Thursday for Jupiter, Friday for Venus, Saturday for Saturn and Rahu.

Table 1.5: Items governed by the nine planets for giving alms (daan)

Planet	Items it governs
Sun	Wheat, *laal chandan, gur* (raw sugar), orange flowers, orange clothes, gold.
Moon	Rice, milk, *safed chandan,* white clothes, silver.
Mars	*Masoor daal*, copper, flower of *kaner,* red clothes.
Mercury	Green fruits, green vegetables, green clothes.
Jupiter	*Chane ki daal*, turmeric, yellow clothes, yellow fruits.
Venus	Diamond, jewellery, ghee, *safed chandan*, white clothes.
Saturn	Iron, *urad daal,* mustard oil, black clothes, shoes.
Rahu	*Sapt dhanya*, lead, *til*, oil, blue clothes.
Ketu	*Til, sapt dhanya,* smoke-coloured clothes, multi-coloured clothes or items and especially black and white clothes.

Propitiating by reciting mantras

Mantras are potent capsules designed to lodge certain required suggestions in the subconscious mind. When a mantra is repeated for a certain number of times then the information sinks into the subconscious mind. The subconscious mind is very powerful and works to implement the vibration-cure to the relevant portion of one's anatomy and cure the ailment over a course of time.

Table 1.6: Mantras for the nine planets

Lord Planet	Mantra
Sun	'Om ghrini suriaye namaha'
Moon	'Om som somaye namaha'
Mars	'Om aum angaarkaye namaha'
Mercury	'Om bum budhaaye namaha'
Jupiter	'Om brim brehespataye namaha'
Venus	'Om shum shukraye namaha'
Saturn	'Om sham shneshcharaye namaha'
Rahu (North node of the Moon)	'Om raang rahvey namaha'
Ketu (South node of the Moon)	'Om kem ketvey namaha'

The above mantras should be recited at the time suggested and for the number of times as per Table 1.7

Table 1.7: Recommended recitation number and preferable time of recitation for mantras for all planets.

Planet	Number of times mantra needs to be recited	Preferable time for recitation
Sun	7,000	Morning
Moon	11,000	Evening
Mars	10,000	Morning
Mercury	9,000	Morning
Jupiter	19,000	Evening
Venus	16,000	Sunrise
Saturn	23,000	Evening
Rahu	18,000	Night
Ketu	17,000	Night

In addition to the above-mentioned mantras for the nine planets we have a treasure of some auspicious mantras, which help cure a disease and recover fast.

Always recite the mantras with concentration and faith.

1. *'Om gan ganpataye namaha'*
This mantra helps cure diseases and remove obstacles. It is suggested that you recite at least two mala (rosary of 108 beads) daily for forty days.

2. *'Shri ramdootaye namaha'*
In order to get freedom from disease, sorrow and difficult times recite at least two mala (rosary of 108 beads) daily for twenty-one days.

3. *'Om triambkam yajamahe sugandhi pushtivardhanam, urvaruk miv bhandhnaat mrityomurkhshiye mamritaat'*

This is known as *mahamritunjai mantra* and is good for recovery from chronic and incurable diseases. Recite at least one mala (rosary of 108 beads) daily for four months.

4. *'Om namaha shivaye'*
By reciting ten mala (rosary of 108 beads) daily for thirty days malefic planets can be propitiated and one gets relief from disease.

Totkaas

Headache: Wrap the root of *majeeth* plant in a cloth and place it on the forehead when there is headache. After it is cured throw the root in the South direction at a road crossing.

Cough: On a Tuesday or a Friday hang around the neck the root of *lobaan* plant; it will cure cough.

Wind troubles: Get a bracelet made of shoe of black horse called *'kale ghore ki naal'* on a Sunday or a Tuesday and wear it.

Diarrhoea: Thread seven equal pieces of *saidai* plant root and tie around the waist.

Stomachache: Hold in hand potable water in a small bowl and recite 108 times the mantra *'Om namaha shivaye'* and drink that water in one go.

Low appetite: To increase appetite lie face down every day for at least an hour.

Epilepsy: Thread twenty-one small pieces of natural salt on a silk thread and wear around the neck.

Note: As this is a serious disease don't just rely on this remedy, also take consultation from a qualified doctor.

Heart diseases: 1. Wear *panch mukhi rudraksh* (five-faced *rudraksh*) in a black thread on a Monday.
2. Offer water to the Sun every morning.

Falling ill repeatedly: Write on a paper the following mantra preferably on a Thursday or a Friday for at least 2,500 times and immerse in running water (river, etc.).
'*Yaa hafeejan, yaa hafeejan, yaa hafeej*'

Diabetes: Take equal quantity of the following:

Shilajeet
Vijay saar
Giloye satt
Gurmaar herb
Chijak

Grind the above very finely and filter and make small tablets of approximately one gram each. Take a tablet twice daily with hot milk for thirty-one days.

Piles: Energise a red thread *(mouli)* with the following mantra and tie it around the big toe.
'*Khurasanki tehni sa, amti amti chal chal swaha*'

Blood pressure: Thread two five-faced and one six-faced *rudraksh* in a black thread and wear it as a necklace.

To regularise menstrual cycle: On a Tuesday boil about six gram pure coriander *(dhania)* in half a litre water. Boil in a brass container till water is reduced to half the original quantity approximately, add about 200-gram sugar to it preferably *mishri*. Starting from a Thursday drink a little of it everyday till Sunday.

www.ingramcontent.com/pod-product-compliance
Lightning Source LLC
Chambersburg PA
CBHW050346030726
47503CB00008B/2634